T0062389

The Black Colonial

Geoff J Gardner

Order this book online at www.trafford.com
or email orders@trafford.com

Most Trafford titles are also available at major online book retailers.

Note for Librarians: A cataloguing record for this book is available from Library and Archives Canada at www.collectionscanada.ca/amicus/index-e.html

Printed in Victoria, BC, Canada.

ISBN: 978-1-4269-1119-4 (Soft)

We at Trafford believe that it is the responsibility of us all, as both individuals and corporations, to make choices that are environmentally and socially sound. You, in turn, are supporting this responsible conduct each time you purchase a Trafford book, or make use of our publishing services. To find out how you are helping, please visit www.trafford.com/responsiblepublishing.html

Our mission is to efficiently provide the world's finest, most comprehensive book publishing service, enabling every author to experience success. To find out how to publish your book, your way, and have it available worldwide, visit us online at www.trafford.com

Trafford rev. 9/10/2009

www.trafford.com

North America & international
toll-free: 1 888 232 4444 (USA & Canada)
phone: 250 383 6864 • fax: 812 355 4082

Acclaim for: The Black Colonial

This is a delightful book that may be read from two different points of view.

In the first place, it is a tale of a young African boy and his subsequent adventures in the wider world.

The other aspect is a story about a young man growing up in an African village, who is corrupted when he travels to the materialistic West.

No matter how you approach the book it is a delightful read, written by a man who has vast knowledge of Africa and Africans.

There is a third approach to this book.

Is this book telling a true story of modern Africa?

You, the reader, may come to your own conclusion.

Colin Bower
International Speaker

Dedications:

To my wife and family for their inspiration.

Acknowledgements:

To Colin Bower for his proof reading and advice.

To Edelgard Kirwin for her proof reading and advice.

To all the oppressed people of the 'Third World' who were the main inspiration for this book.

The Black Colonial

1

With a scream from his mother, a slap from the acting mid-wife and a cry, Antonio Thica entered the world, the first son and heir of the High Chief of Cobuki.

His arrival was welcomed by the whole village and many others had travelled from the neighbouring villages to witness this great event.

The High Chief Malanda Thica, a man educated by life, his father, the Elders of the village and the occasional Monk who would arrive at the village unannounced and leave when he thought his work was done, had only been the High Chief for a short time since his father had died some two months earlier. He was a proud man who had been given all the luxury that could be afforded from a small village at that time in the Northern Province of Romanbasque. This consisted mainly of being able to choose his own bride from any of the females in the village or even another village if he chooses to, and not having to till the land or fish with the other men from the village. Quite a highly respected lifestyle and the envy of all others who had their wives chosen for them by their families depending on the amount of potential brides that were available and the dowry the family of the bride could offer for the benefit of having a husband.

Malanda took his son from his wife and showed him around as if he had just received a long awaited present. "O filho da mudança The Son of Change" he would say as he offered Antonio to all that had assembled.

Malanda had plans for his 'New Born,' for the 'buzz word' within Romanbasque was now 'EDUCATION.'

Education was something that was relatively new to this area, well in the form of what we as Europeans understand it anyway.

Education as previously known of and expected in Cobuki was that of how to prepare the land to produce the best crops in time for harvest or, how to look after the animals to be able to produce the best yields of milk or meat to eat and fish.

The education Malanda had in mind for his son Antonio was that of the Western European type, school, college and later on to a good University, the type of education that would be the envy of all the neighbours for many kilometres around. An education that could be used to bring wealth and prosperity to his people and his neighbours to ensure their development for the future and show Malanda as a man who cared for his people by allowing his son to lead the way forward. That would make Antonio a great leader for his people when it was his turn to become their Chief when Malanda would no longer be with them.

Education in the area in which they lived was a fairly new thing to be bestowed on them, well, in the modern sense of the word. For the last few hundred years from time to time a Jesuit Monk would turn up in the village and commence to teach the current teachings of the Catholic Church. They would also convert as many of the locals to Catholicism as they could and in fact the Jesuit Monks over the years done a very good job within the whole of Romanbasque as far as the Catholic faith was concerned.

What Malanda's idea was that he would be taking full advantage of the schooling being offered by the Charities based within Romanbasque who were now offering an education in the European way from teachers who themselves come from Europe and some from America.

Schools were starting to be set up all over Romanbasque, even in the outlining villages and although Malanda himself didn't know too much of this new education, he knew it was something very special that his son would need for the future.

Malanda's first aim was to get one of these schools into his village and to do that, he had formulated a plan. He would have one of these school rooms built and furnish it with all of its needs. He would make contact with a Charity and ensure that they knew what facilities he had in his village and that they were ready for a school to be started.

He would have accommodation built befitting a European to live in that would have as many things in it that any European would be very comfortable living there. To enable him to get the right information he would send someone out to the City where he knew of magazines being sold with pictures of these things in them. From these magazines he would start a shopping list and over the time from now to when Antonio would need to start his school he would ensure that all requirements would be made available for both the school room and the teacher's accommodation.

Malanda knew that this would not be a small task but he had time and the time would be used wisely to ensure his aim would be realised in good time before the school education for his son would need to start.

His plan would be put into action as soon as he had a chance to speak with the Village Elders to get their agreement to back the plan. This agreement he was quite sure he would get from them as they would always back Malanda, they thought greatly of his wise decisions and never before had he had anything vetoed by them.

Malanda arranged a meeting with Elders for the following week, but in the meantime he didn't waste any time thinking of what he would say to them.

He would walk out of the village alone, sometimes for many hours at a time and speak aloud to himself practicing every word until he had it to perfection. This being the only option for a man who could not read or write and was incapable of writing anything down that he could edit as he went along.

The meeting drew near and Malanda went over in his mind one final time exactly what he wanted to put over to the Elders. However, when he entered the meeting one of the Elders stood up and said

'Malanda you're right and you have our full backing.' Malanda was struck dumb just for that moment.

'How do you know what I was going to say?'

It was explained to him that during his many strolls out into the bush alone it was not hard to hear from the close proximity of the other villagers working in the immediate area. It had been the topic of their conversation for the last few days and they were more than happy to go along with a school for their children, grand children and many lines of their children's children to come.

Malanda, very relieved, set about outlining his plan of attack to the Elders and very soon he was being given other very good suggestions to add to his list of requirements.

The meeting went on for many hours into the night and at every turn the plan got better and more in depth than even Malanda would have imagined would happen.

It was decided that one person would be in control of this great list, the name they had given to it. They had it compiled in words and that job was given to the only Elder who could himself already read and write, if not at any great standard. He had been taught by one of the travelling Monks during a very bad illness of Malaria he had suffered and the Monk had spent a great deal of time nursing him back to good health. He was ill for a long duration of more than eleven months and the Monk taught him to read and write during their long hours together.

'Tamo the Educated' as he was affectionately known as from that point on, started to write the great list, also he inserted names of the persons responsible for each section of the list and gave them periods of time in which they should report their progress to the others. I suppose Tamo would have been one of the first Project Managers in this Northern village of Romanbasque.

Included in the great list was an inventory of all items they would need and also the magazines they would need to identify the extra's to make any European feel truly at home in this far reaching part of the world.

The day following the meeting everyone was very excited and their new school room was the talk of the village. There were no doubts in anyone's mind that this was the best plan that Malanda had come up with for a very long time, even to the point that it was the best plan the village had ever worked on.

It was decided that two men would leave the village the following week and make their way on foot for the 600 kilometre walk to the City. The two men were chosen and Tamo was given the job of thoroughly briefing them on what was expected from them for their task.

Tamo would go over and repeat their task many times and before they both left they were fully conversant as to what was expected of them, and exactly what they had to bring back with them.

Money was gathered from different families around the village and the sum of $4.20 and 102,000 Romanbasque Reticalie were collected a total of about £5.00 in British Sterling.

It doesn't seem a lot from a whole village but the harvest had not been brought in as yet and the fishing the village done was for their daily requirements and that was what was left from last year's money. From now on it would get even harder money wise for all in the village, as they all had as their main aim the school room and their very own teacher. They had in the past, in their own way, had to pull up their socks and tighten their belts but this time it would be even harder but they were sure they could make it happen and more importantly they all wanted to make it happen.

2

Limpo and Garro, the two men chosen to make the trip to the City, left the village to a great cheer from all the other villagers and they left with a sense of pride with them for being chosen from all the other men in the village.

They had been given supplies for their trip and were also given plenty of farewell kisses which they really enjoyed, especially from the single ladies as both Limpo and Garro had not yet chosen a wife.

They made their way across the bush and it wasn't long before the village was out of sight and they knew they were now well and truly on their mission.

As they walked they began a conversation of testing each other on the duties of their task. It was a long way to go but they would be sure not to forget a single item from their memorised list, they had been given the privilege to complete.

They tested each for what seemed like hours but it had only been just three hours when they decided to stop for a rest break.

Garro opened one of the packs he had been carrying and to his amazement he was looking at a full crusted meat pie. This type of food was only normally seen at a top celebration in their village and the sense of pride again hit him very hard. He showed the pie to Limpo and they both shared the pride to the point that a real sense of responsibility hit them and they wrapped up the pie in Garro's pack and continued on their way.

It was many hours later that they thought they had done enough for that day and it was now dark so they settled down to make camp for the night.

Their first taste of that pie was fantastic and they enjoyed it and later had some more, they then settled down to sleep for a few hours.

This routine continued throughout their journey and their diet was supplemented by berries and root plants they gathered as they travelled along.

One morning Limpo had risen early and gone for a stroll and left his friend lying for a while longer. Shortly after Garro awoke and as he pushed himself up into the sitting position he found himself face to face with a 'Spitting Cobra.' Garro froze and he could feel the blood draining away from his face. Just as he could feel the Cobra was going to spit the snake disappeared. Limpo had returned and arrived at the scene just as Garro was sitting up. A firm grasp, a sharp tug of the Cobra's tail, a lash and the Cobra would be on their menu that night and possibly for a couple of nights to come. The spittle was soon dripped away from that snake in grass.

Situation relieved and the pair were soon packed up, snake and all and again on their merry way.

Limpo and Garro had known each other since their births and had spent a lot of time together over the years but not for periods as long as this one. It was obvious that at times on the route they would have the occasional disagreement but not these two. They had just one thing on their minds and the sense of responsibility was overwhelming that nothing else got in its way.

If one of them made a decision the other would automatically follow without question. They continued in harmony and became even better friends than either had thought possible just a week before.

As they walked they started to make promises to each other. If one had a problem succeeding in his part of the mission the other would assist him. They would make oaths that this was their mission, not either as an individual and they would both work to ensure that the whole mission was completed.

This mission was so important to them and they knew it would make a big difference to their status within the village on their return, having successfully completed it. All the young ladies would see them as heroes and this would make their choice for wives' a lot easier as they could choose someone who normally would be out of their reach due to their current standing in the pecking order of the village.

Many days passed and early on the ninth day, they were crossing a hilly and rocky terrain when on reaching the top of one of its crests they saw in the distance the outline of the City of Nompulari.

Nompulari, the third City of Romanbasque is situated in the Northern Region of the Country approximately 200 kilometres from the East Coast and the Indian Ocean.

It took them a few more hours to reach the outskirts of the City and as they approached it they both had a sense of anxiety as it was their first ever visit to such a Metropolis. They had seen pictures in some magazines of what a City looked like and from the magazine it all seemed very exciting but now they were experiencing the reality of being there and they felt strange.

Questions started to come from Limpo

"Would they be accepted by the locals?

Would they be able to make themselves understood due to their dialect?

Would their mission now be in jeopardy?"

Garro felt the same way but decided to be strong and offered words of encouragement to his friend. They entered the big City and took their chance.

It was still strange for them both as they entered Nompulari. Huge buildings greeted them, which neither had ever seen before. They were only used to the single storey mud huts that surrounded their village back home. This was their first ever encounter with multi storey buildings that seemed to go up and up. In fact the average building only raised three or four storeys.

They met a man, who gave his name as Giuseppe. A typically, poorly dressed African man, who was sat on the ground begging. They felt quite safe talking to him as he was dressed similar to them.

Giuseppe, they found out was also from a distant village away from Nompulari and had been in the City for about two years. He had come here alone after losing his wife to an illness and was hoping to get a new start in life. He said that he was wearing the same clothes that he had come in, that is all apart from his shorts, which he had found on the street a few months earlier. His business as he put it was doing quite well and after a slow start in the early days he now had a clientele that could realise him at least 20,000 Romanbasque Reticalie a day as long as he was prepared to put the hours in. Many very poor Africans will do this type of work when there is nothing else to be had. If they can afford the materials they will also set up as a shoe shine and could make a little more money, but this takes capital to start up, which most don't have. Anyway Giuseppe was managing on his income so had no reason to change.

The lads had arrived, unbeknown to them late on a Sunday and Giuseppe informed them that all the places they would need to visit would be closed for today. They felt a bit let down as that would mean they would lose a day in their task but I supposed that will allow them time to find somewhere to stay while they were here.

A big smile came over both their faces when their new found friend said

"You can stay with me. I have to finish my shift, so go and

have a look around and I'll meet you back here when it starts to get dark."

Happy with what they had accomplished, they both went on their ways to take in the big City for their first time.

What a start, they had found a friend and they had accommodation for the night, and if they kept Giuseppe sweet they would probably have accommodation for as long as they needed it. They both were now feeling more settled than they had expected to feel and off they went to try and locate where they would start their mission when the shops opened the following day.

Remembering the location they had left Giuseppe they walked up one street and there they were. A whole line of shops selling everything they had imagined they would sell during their trip to Nompulari. They looked in each shop, gazing in at the wonderful things in their windows. They were both amazed at what was available to be bought and they spoke about what a wonderful accommodation they would be able to provide for their villages teacher. They looked at the items in awe but at this time failed to realise what all this would cost. They didn't feel the need at this point and just took in all what they could see.

They must have spent at least five hours window shopping when the darkness started to come and they decided it was time to go back and find Giuseppe.

They hadn't wondered far, they had only looked down one street so they were back with their friend after just a few minutes.

Giuseppe had already packed up his patch of a blanket, which he had been sitting on, a bowl not unlike a small fruit bowl and his sign that said he was a war victim. Most people in this area had time for war victims and Giuseppe had learnt this soon after his arrival in Nompulari. This had given him the marketing plan he needed for success of his business.

The three friends walked off down the other way from the

shopping area and ended up in a short lane behind a restaurant. This Giuseppe explained was his home and everything he had were now theirs to enjoy. The lads thanked him and wondered what they could have to eat for it had been a long time since they had last eaten. Garro looked in the pack and there was still some pie left, amazingly after their long journey and a good quantity of fruit. He laid it out and all three of them tucked in to a variable feast for their evening meal.

After their meal Giuseppe disappeared for a few minutes and returned with a bottle of beer. He opened it and it was passed around so they all could taste its flavour. The three of them were getting on fine and soon after the beer bottle was empty they settled down to sleep.

Giuseppe's blanket was put out on the concrete upon some old boxes that he had kept hidden behind a bin. More cardboard was used for cover but it was still relatively warm about 22oC so that wasn't needed that evening.

The two newcomers slept for about eight hours, which was a long time for them but after their long journey they obviously needed it. Giuseppe was already gone when they awoke so they tidied away the boxes and blanket in hand made their way down to where they knew Giuseppe would be.

It didn't take them very long and they could soon see their friend at his patch trying to make a small living.

"Hi" said Limpo from a distance and Giuseppe stood and waved quite vigorously at his two companions as they neared him.

"Did you have a good sleep?" asked Giuseppe.

"Yes thanks" the two lads replied and they joined Giuseppe sat at his patch after laying the blanket down for each of them to share.

"I came out a bit earlier this morning knowing I would have extra mouths to feed this evening" Giuseppe said.

The boys thanked him but said it was OK they were in a position to pay their own way.

"What do you have then?" asked Giuseppe.

Garro opened the pack and produced the total of their funds so Giuseppe could see for himself.

"That money you will need for your mission, you're in my City and it is up to me to look after my friends when their in town."

Giuseppe said with a sound of pride in his voice that he was for the first time since arriving in Nompulari, entertaining. You would do the same for me if I was passing through your village, I just know you would" Giuseppe said.

The lads thanked Giuseppe for his kindness, bid him farewell for the day and made their way back towards the shopping area.

Not only were the shops open, but many people had joined the scene, which only yesterday had been so quiet and empty as they had done their window shopping.

The first shop they went to was a Newsagent, which they didn't in fact know that this was what it was called but it did have in its window the magazines they were looking to buy. They entered the store and from the shelves took several magazines down to investigate the pictures inside them.

The first seemed only to be full of tubs, but they did like the look of the ladies who were posing near these objects. They didn't recognised the baths as they had never seen one before but thought that it really wasn't an item they would need for the teachers accommodation.

The next one they looked at was better. It had tables and chairs and beds and blankets, this they knew they would need. As a start they decided to buy just this one and take it back with them so that Giuseppe could give his advice having lived in the City and had a greater knowledge of how other people live and what they need.

Limpo took the magazine to the counter and said,

"I would like to buy this one!"

The shop assistant took the magazine from him, turned it over to see the price on the back cover and announced,

"$2.00 please."

Garro opened the pack once again and took out the cloth in which he had been carrying the money. Not being used to handling money he offered the cloth to the assistant so she could help herself. She took out a $1.00 coin and the rest was made up of 5 and 10 cent pieces.

Outside the shop they were very happy with their purchase and looked through it again before the realization took hold of what it had actually cost them. The price was nearly half their total funds and it was only one magazine.

Near anxiety rocked the lads as they made their way off to speak to their friend Giuseppe, and explain to him what had just happened.

They neared their friend but hung back for a while as he was busy with a customer and they talked for about five minutes in all before the lads could get near to speak with him.

"Giuseppe! We have a problem that hopefully you will be able to advise us about."

Garro outlined what had happened and was near to exhaustion when Giuseppe said,

"STOP!"

The person Giuseppe had been talking to was a wealthy owner in the City and Giuseppe had got to know him quite well. He had been telling him all about his two new friends that had arrived in the City just yesterday and had told him about what they were looking to achieve while they were here.

The Gent had been very interested in what he had been told and had invited them all to his apartment that evening to talk about it and to see in what way he would be able to assist them.

Limpo and Garro were slightly relieved but still upset about all the money they had just spent on their one item. Giuseppe told them he had known this man for a long time now and he was one of the better people who always stop and pass the time of day with him. The lads seemed to calm a bit but Giuseppe could still see it in their faces for the next few hours.

All three friends sat for the rest of the day at Giuseppe's patch and talked and laughed and really got to know each other just that bit better.

The end of the working day neared as the sun faded and was replaced by the darkness. This process in Romanbasque can take a very little time and in only minutes it was dark and they packed up the patch and made their way back to Giuseppe's place to prepare for their meeting that evening.

They safely packed away what they wouldn't need for their meeting and made their way off Giuseppe taking the lead. It was only a short walk to the Gent's apartment and number three was pressed on the panel of bells at the porch.

It was only seconds when a voice spoke asking who was there.

"Giuseppe Sir" was the response and the buzzer sounded to allow them to enter the building. This was all new to Limpo and Garro and as they walked following Giuseppe their eyes were everywhere, taking everything in, on the short walk up the stairs to the apartment. In the entry to the building was a fine table with one chair and on top of the table were many magazines just like the one they had bought that day. Pictures of animal scenes adorned each wall as they turned the stairs to ascend its flights, but what were so interesting to them both were the colours. Each wall was a different bright colour of red, orange, lime green and yellow. To them they had entered a palace and they were now going to meet the King.

The door to the apartment was open and as they neared a call came out,

"Come in boys."

They entered the apartment into a hallway, again in rich colour with a large picture of the African Big Five, which are the Lion, Elephant, Rhino, Buffalo and Leopard painted on it. A few steps more and they were in what felt like to them, a church. They had entered a large room with a big open space in the middle and what seemed to be very comfortable seats around the walls. The Gent they had come to see joined the boys after coming from the left and another room and very confidently put his hand out to welcome them all.

"Hi Stephan, Stephan Green."

The boys replied with their names and Stephan invited them all to sit down.

Stephan Green was a tall, well built, white South African and he was in Nompulari as he ran a business from here. Garro imagined that he had something in common with Mr. Green as the only photograph he could see was one of a much older couple who would possibly be his parents but no photos of a younger lady or children. Garro took it that Mr. Green had also not yet chosen a wife for himself.

Stephan had run his business in Nompulari for just over five years and he was in the jewellery trade, selling high class necklaces made from mainly gold but also platinum. He got on well with the Romanbasque's, especially the not so lucky as he had also had to work very hard starting as a child to get where is was today, and he had literally started with nothing.

Made an orphan at just 12 years of age, with no other family to care for him, he had also landed on the street as a beggar.

He had worked the streets for four years until one day he found a gold necklace. He was down on his luck but his morals were still in-tacked so he had taken the necklace to the police.

The policeman he reported it to, just laughed.

"This isn't gold son."

The policeman said.

"It is just an old piece of tin and I can't see anyone wanting that back, you have it and good luck to you."

Stephan thought to himself, well at least I had thought I was doing the right thing but if he isn't interested someone else maybe.

He took the necklace to a pawn broker and was given $15.00 for it. He was up on his luck and he was not going to go down again.

With the $15.00 he bought some smaller trinkets and back on the street he found they were selling quite well. With the profits he bought some more and the rest is history and it had made him into the successful businessman he is today.

"Tea anyone or would you prefer a cold drink?"

All three answered simultaneously with

"Cold please"

And Stephan opened a fridge in the corner of the room and gave them all an orange drink.

"Help yourselves to nuts" he announced.

"So, I have been thinking over what Giuseppe had told me today about why you are in town and I think I might be in a position to help you boys out," Stephan said.

"I believe you have come here to gather magazines so you can work out what you might need for your new teacher," he continued.

Limpo immediately jumped in and said that

"One or two of the old magazines downstairs would do if you could spare them."

Giuseppe translated for all of them as the village lads didn't speak the way the townies spoke, and the conversation was a lot slower than I can portray in this account.

Stephan laughed and said,

"Magazines you are talking about, you are so humble from the villages. I am talking of what you find in the magazines."

Limpo, Garro and even Giuseppe looked puzzled and waited for Stephan to explain what he was saying.

"I have to leave Nompulari shortly for at least a two year period and when I return, if I had all my furniture put into storage quite possibly it would be in a bad state of repair with all the humidity and the like and I would just have to get all new."

"So what are you saying Mr. Stephan" asked Giuseppe.

"You can have it, all of it; whatever you wish to have it's yours," said Stephan.

Giuseppe took his time to explain what Stephan was saying and it took a while for it all to sink in, but when it had they just sat, silent, motionless for what seemed like an age.

The three lads looked at each other in disbelief and Giuseppe thought to himself that he couldn't have even imagined when he was talking to Stephan today that tonight would turn out anything like this. He was pleased that he had met Stephan today but more, he was very pleased he had been able to help out his two new friends in such a spectacular way.

Limpo announced

"We've done it, we have achieved our mission, all because of a friend we met or who God himself had sent us to. God bless you Mr. Stephan, God bless you Giuseppe, God bless you."

3

Stephan Green would be leaving Nompulari in about two months time so the lads had to get things arranged with their village to get all this houseful of furniture back to the village.

The three friends thanked Stephan and made their way back to Giuseppe's place. All the way there they were silent and pondering of what had just happened. Limpo and Garro had a beaming smile on their faces tinted with a look of amazement.

When they had settled down after placing the blanket down and getting the boxes out, Garro began to talk. "What a wonderful night it has been, what a lovely person that was, we are surely blessed by meeting him through our friend Giuseppe."

Limpo agreed, and for the first time Giuseppe seemed to be embarrassed. The rest of the evening was spent talking about the events of that nights meeting and wondering what the reception would be on their return to their village with the great news.

Limpo and Garro agreed that they would start their way back to the village first thing in the morning after a good night's sleep. Sleeping was the last thing they all wanted to do due to the excitement they felt, and it was very late when they eventually settled down but not before they had drank a full bottle of beer each in way of celebration.

The three lads' slept, but only until dawn and Limpo and Garro got up quickly and prepared to make their way home.

They both thanked Giuseppe for all his help and friendship and promised to be back as soon as they could. Giuseppe wished them a safe and speedy return home and an even quicker return to Nompulari for he knew he would miss them both so much.

The three of them walked together to the outskirts of the City, hugged, shock hands and parted. Giuseppe watched their progress until what must have been an hour later, when they disappeared out of view. Giuseppe felt quite exhausted as all the time his friends had been walking away from him he had been waving to them and shouting words of encouragement as they went on their way.

* * * *

The journey home was uneventful and they made good time, running when they had the energy.

About a kilometre from the village they were spotted and they could just hear the dull drone of a call going out through the village. As the drone became clearer they saw a small gathering of villagers, which was being added to the nearer they got to them.

"It's Limpo and Garro returning" they could hear, and they still had a few hundred metres to go. One person broke from the gathering and started running towards them. It turned out to be Garro's younger brother Simon who approached them with a big smile on his face to see his brother and friend back.

"Garro" Simon shouted as he ran towards them in full excitement.

"Garro, Limpo you're back" he continued as he arrived at the two travellers.

All the boys embraced and made their way to join the crowd which had now assembled to wait for them.

At the front of the crowd was Chief Malanda who also embraced the boys and hoped they had plenty of good things to tell him about their travels. The two friends said they had lots of news and were ready to start telling the Chief as soon as he was ready to hear what they had to say.

"First, return to your families, greet your parents and then we will speak."

The lad's thanked the Chief and they arranged to meet up in his hut as soon as dark came.

Malanda arranged for the Elders to be at his hut for the traveller's news, and instructed his wife to prepare food for his guests.

Soon after dark, Limpo and his father Isaac who was himself an Elder walked in unannounced into the Chief's hut. As soon as Isaac spoke Malanda looked towards Limpo and beckoned him to join him at his side. Garro arrived soon after and he also joined the Chief at the front of the gathering.

Not to seem too pushy, Malanda first asked the lad's about their journey and he listened with interest as they described how the journey had gone. Malanda sat patient, but it was obvious he was only being polite. Then Garro got to the part when they had arrived in Nompulari and the atmosphere changed and excitement was suddenly in the air.

They told of their meeting with their good friend Giuseppe who would become their saviour after they had themselves made a bad mistake. The atmosphere dulled a little as the news seemed to be going in the wrong direction for the Elders'. Limpo noticed this, and thought it was the right time to produce their purchase of the magazine.

A gasp went through the hut as if they had produced the 'Holy Grail' and once again they had everybody's attention. People rose from their seats to get closer to the magazine and Limpo started to open each page to show off their prize.

After several 'flicking's' of the magazine Limpo said

"This is what we have arranged to get from Nompulari."

"Yes, that is what we would like to get" Malanda said,

"But we must first have organised what money we will need."

Once again Limpo stated his fact and Garro was not slow to reiterate it. The Chief tried to explain but the boys stopped him and said they had more to add to their story.

'What we have to tell you is what we believe to be a miracle.' Said Garro

The two boys told their story of Giuseppe and meeting Mr. Stephan and the visit to Mr. Stephan's home and that Mr. Stephan must leave Nompulari and eventually they got to the part where they told of all his furniture he was willing to let the village have for their own.

A deathly silence came over the hut and just like professional orators Limpo and Garro paused for effect.

It was a while before someone spoke and the speaker was Isaac, Limpo's father.

"Are you sure you have understood this Gentleman son? People don't just give away a whole load of their furniture. Now have you got this absolutely right?"

Garro told the Elder's exactly what had happened and that they had to collect it as soon as they could. Giuseppe would meet us there, and that anyone who made the trip could stay at Giuseppe's place for the night.

"We thank you for your time in doing this great thing, but we need to talk now, so leave us, and we will speak again tomorrow."

The two lad's left the hut and were stopped by the Chief's wife Ammanni,

"You must eat before you leave" she said, and she showed them over to a trestle table she had prepared that was full of food.

Garro was first to help himself and took a large portion of rice and a tomato and onion based sauce. He thanked Ammanni and sat a short distance away on the trunk of a felled tree to eat it. He was soon after joined by Limpo and the two lads' wondered what was being said inside the hut in their absence.

Limpo would be surprised if they even believed their story but Garro as always was more confident and as soon as he had finished his meal he set off, telling Limpo to join him when he had finished.

Garro was at another hut talking to its owner.

"Can we have your barrow?"

Garro asked Georgio who was very proud of the barrow as he was the only person in the village who had one.

"Yes of course" Georgio said.

"What are you doing with it?"

Garro explained that they would need more than one barrow to collect all the furniture from Nompulari and he was taking it to Markus the carpenter to ask him to make at least two more.

Markus looked at the barrow after Garro had told him what he wanted him to do and after a while he said,

"Wheels, we will need wheels. I can make the barrows but we don't have any wheels in the village, so if you can get me the wheels I can make the barrows without any problem."

Now, if Westerners wanted some wheels, they would just go down to the local scrap yard and buy some, not in Africa, in a remote village. They would have to find someone who had some that weren't doing anything, or find a large enough tree from which the wheel shapes could be cut from its trunk.

Garro and Limpo decided on the latter, and would go out early in the morning to find such a tree.

They were making their way back to their own huts when Limpo's father shouted to them to rejoin them in the Chief's hut.

As they entered it was obvious to them that their story had been believed, as all the Elders started to pat them on their backs and cheer. Malanda took the lead by saying,

"We will be starting work tomorrow on working out how to get the furniture back to the village" but Garro butted in.

"Chief we have already started and Markus the carpenter will be making some barrows to carry the furniture on. Limpo and I have to get the tree for him tomorrow morning from which he will be able to cut the wheels."

The Chief praised their drive but added that they would now get help from the others.

"So, let us eat!" said Malanda,

And once again Limpo and Garro helped themselves to a large portion of rice and sauce. The night was a success and the boy's felt good having such splendid remarks made about them.

In the morning there were many men available for the work that had to be done and Tamo was organising them into work parties. Some were sent to help Markus with the building of the barrows and others to help get the tree so the wheels could be cut from it. For the next few days it was a definite case of busy in the village, notwithstanding the extra attention Limpo and Garro were getting from the unattached females who were really taking a great interest in them both. They were now a lot more special in the village than before they had gone on their great adventure.

As all the work was done, Malanda, Tamo and some of the Elders were looking through the magazine and deciding what they would like and Tamo was writing a list which he would take with him to Nompulari and, as the furniture was loaded he would tick off what was already on their list.

Also they discussed the building of the teacher's accommodation and it was decided that would commence as soon as possible so they could put the goods from Nompulari straight into it on their return.

As they all spoke about what needed to be done Joseph, one of the Elders started pacing out where he thought the building should be sited. He had built many of the huts already in the village so he had taken the lead on this one.

The only main difference to any normal construction in the village is that this building wouldn't be round, but oblong.

Women would be put to work to gather rushes to plait them into the roof parts. Plenty of small trees would have to cut to make the wall struts. Lots of work would have to be done and now in a very short time to accommodate everything they would be bringing back with them.

Everything that had to happen was well thought out and all was starting to happen. The barrows were completed in record time. The building was taking shape and the party who would go to Nompulari had been chosen and a day was set for them to leave.

Of course, Limpo and Garro would be taking the lead but also Malanda had also chosen to go with them. A party of about twenty were organised and the final preparations for their departure were made by packing food and water for the trip.

Then at the end of one day's work, and just before everybody made their way back to their own huts, Malanda announced that they would be leaving the next day as soon as it became light. A cheer went out as if the village was just about to go into battle and there was a great sense of excitement in the air. People started to dance and hug each other, and someone even started to beat out a tune on a drum. The villagers were happy and nobody was going to stop them celebrating, and this euphoria continued for the next few hours.

4

When all the goodbyes had been said, which took rather longer than would normally be expected, the team set off with Limpo, Garro and Chief Malanda leading.

Good time was made crossing the bush and they made it into Nompulari on the morning of the tenth day, sometimes pulling, sometimes pushing the barrows along with them.

Limpo and Garro wasted no time at all in locating their friend Giuseppe and the happy trio hugged and jumped with the joy at being together again.

Giuseppe was introduced to Malanda and the rest of the team and after packing up Giuseppe's business things they all made their way off to an open grassed area to speak.

Giuseppe told them that it wouldn't be until that evening when he could go and talk to Mr. Stephan so they had plenty of time to all get to know each other. Malanda tried to get answers from Giuseppe to the many questions he had, but of course Giuseppe wasn't in a position to answer any of them. He just said that he had known Mr. Stephan for a time that he was a nice man and he was prepared to help the village. Giuseppe also reassured the Chief that he had in fact seen and spoken to Mr. Stephan that morning, so he is still in town.

The rest of the day was spent with the trio catching up and some of the others going for walks around the City. For nearly all of them, it was the first time that they had been to a City. Malanda had visited Nompulari many years before with his parents but it had changed a great deal since then, so even he was interested to have a look around.

They had arranged to meet back at the grassed area as it got dark and sure enough as the light started to fade bodies from the team turned up.

It was decided that only Malanda, Giuseppe, Limpo and Garro would go to Mr. Stephan's apartment and all the rest would wait for them to return.

When they entered Mr. Stephan's apartment most of his personnel belongings had been packed into boxes and were sat in the middle of the big room.

Giuseppe had done the introductions and Malanda told Mr. Stephan of how lucky they all felt and that how they were blessed by his generosity.

Stephan gave them some reasons as to why he was willing to help them but most of it fell on deaf ears as they could only see him as their savoiur and didn't want to hear excuses. They were so privileged to have had such a benefactor.

Stephan said that he would be leaving in about a week's time but for the rest of his time in Nompulari he would be going into an hotel. If they wanted to start taking things out first thing in the morning, that would be ok by him.

Malanda made sure to invite Mr. Stephan to his village and really hoped that he could find the time one day to come and see them. The boy's added,

"You will visit Mr. Stephan, please come and see us."

Stephan promised that he would but for now he had a dinner engagement to go to so he must leave them.

Back with the others Malanda told them all what would be happening and they then followed Giuseppe back to his place to spend the night.

There was still plenty of food left for their trip back, as enough food had been prepared that would have probably lasted them all a month so they sat down and had a good meal, some bottles of beer were also shared around before settling down to sleep.

At first light everybody was awake and ready for a day's works. Giuseppe and Malanda led the way with three barrows being pulled behind the rest of the team.

They arrived at Stephan's apartment and Giuseppe rang the bell and waited, and waited and waited some more. Giuseppe rang the bell again. They stood waiting for five or more minutes ringing the bell several times until eventually Stephan's voice was heard over the speaker, "Hello who's that?"

"Hi Mr. Stephan it's Giuseppe."

Stephan pressed the buzzer to release the door and they entered the building.

When they arrived at the apartment door they found Stephan stood there just laughing, for whilst they couldn't understand what he was laughing at, they joined in with the laughing anyway.

Once they had all calmed down Stephan said it wasn't a problem but what he was laughing at was the time.

When you normally make arrangements to meet someone first thing in the morning, people take it that you mean eight or nine o'clock. However, when you arrange to meet an African villager first thing in the morning, they take it as being when it is first light. The time was now just 4.00 AM.

Stephan told them to come in and this was loud enough for all to hear and they all started to make their way into his apartment. It wasn't long before Malanda realised the problem and said that the only people he wanted in the apartment was Limpo, Garro, Tamo and Giuseppe, the rest of you wait outside in the street until I call you.

Stephan excused himself and went into the kitchen to put his morning coffee on.

"Anyone like a drink?" Stephan asked.

Malanda said he would but the others seemed to decline politely.

"I need my coffee first thing in the morning or I don't seem to be ready for the day." Stephan said.

Malanda never usually had coffee back in the village and couldn't remember the last time he had drank it, but he was looking forward to having some, especially with such a special person.

"The only things I don't want you to take are in the boxes, you will find some in most rooms but they are all going with me." Stephan instructed.

"You can make a start if you like while the Chief and I have our coffee."

Tamo took out his list and started to tick items that were on it and the others made their way downstairs with the first of many loads.

As he was ticking his list Tamo's face had a lovely smile on it as nearly everything he had listed was here and it was now theirs. The joy he was experiencing was a wonderful sight and it was noticed by the others.

"We won't have much to get once we have this lot back to the village." Stephan heard what he was saying and added,

"It's a pleasure to know where it will be going and that it is going to be appreciated."

Tamo chuckled

"Thank you sir."

When the last of the furniture left the apartment Stephan and the Chief went downstairs together to see the result of the loading. It was all on and the three barrows had been required but as Stephan looked at the loads he thought,

"There's something missing?"

Malanda looked for himself but couldn't see what Mr. Stephan thought was missing.

"Have we missed something Mr. Stephan?"

"Not as much missed something Chief but there is something missing, rope. If you try and move these barrows without roping it on the loads will just fall off."

"Rope Tamo." The Chief said.

Tamo looked at the Chief in the 'we haven't got any' look, which was understood by everyone.

"I'll sort it Chief" Giuseppe shouted and sped off to somewhere because he was around the corner of the apartment block and gone before anyone was able to reply, even if they had wanted too.

Giuseppe was away for about ten minutes but when he returned he had various thicknesses and various lengths of rope, twine and cord. He issued them out to anyone near him and they began to sort out the ties so they could secure the loads.

The loads were secured and the long trek back to the village began. Malanda bid Stephan farewell and again thanked him very much and said he looked forward to seeing Mr. Stephan in his village very soon. Stephan wished them all well and the convoy set off.

They hadn't travelled very far when they stopped to say goodbye to Giuseppe who they all thanked personally. This process took more than ten minutes and eventually they were off again. Slow, steady but underway.

The trip back to Cobuki would be painstaking and arduous at times, but they all knew it was for the best, so kept going as best they could.

Everything was going well for a few days and then one wheel fell off. On checking it wasn't that the wheel had just fallen off the axle had broken, and here they were in the middle of the African Bush and not a tree in sight for the present. It would be another two days before the came across a tree so in the meantime they took it in turns to hold up the axle while turning the barrow only on the other wheel. It was slow but they were very determined.

It took a total of fifteen days to get back to the village and all the men on the trip, including Malanda had worked hard and they were to say the least extremely tired on their return. They had also returned very late at night so nobody was there waiting for them or welcoming them home. When they had got all three barrows under some sort of cover for the night, Malanda just sent everybody home until the morning; he for one needed some sleep and was sure the other's would feel the same.

5

Morning began late for the team of barrow boys, and it was eight o'clock when they eventually were all outside to get the barrows emptied. Before they started they took a look at the piece of land where the teacher's accommodation was going to be built and just couldn't believe their eyes.

The accommodation had been finished. It had been started, built and completed by the few men left behind and the women of the village.

"It is superb." Malanda said, with a triumphant roar.

The new accommodation was a large oblong walled building measuring about ten metres long and five metres wide. It had been constructed using the 'Wattle and Daub' method of construction. This method is where the walls are first laced with reeds between saplings about a metre apart and then a mixture of mud and straw are layered on to the reeds from both sides and then left to bake in the sun. A very substantial structure is the final result using this method. The roof was all made of plaited reeds and plants from the bush had been planted around its outside walls. Malanda entered, and was quickly followed by someone with a lantern.

"What a place, a lovely place for anyone to stay and enjoy their time in."

From idea's they had got from the magazine, windows had been put into the walls, but without any actual windows, but shutters had been made for the outside of the windows. Even a path about three metres long had been put in using stones leading from the front door. Inside there was nothing but emptiness, so Malanda took this as the cue to get everything unloaded and into the house.

It didn't take long to loosen the ties from the barrows and the unloading began. Each item was first placed on the ground just outside the house and then Tamo would tell the carriers where it was to be put inside the house.

This continued for a few items before Ammanni stepped forward and in a trice, took over. A fairly small woman certainly compared to her husband but more than capable to get the job done.

"Men just haven't got a clue," she muttered, and some other wives stepped forward to help her.

"We'll do this, you lot go and make yourselves busy elsewhere" she ordered

And with a glance of disapproval from Malanda who looked at her strained as he had certainly never been pushed out by his wife before this occasion. He understood she meant business though, and he led the other men off to basically get them out of the women's way.

From where the men were sitting they could hear a real hive of activity going on inside the house with various voices taking the lead as the work progressed. It was only about twenty minutes when the women called the men back over to take a look at what they done.

Malanda was the first to enter and he was really impressed with how he found the house, all laid out and looking very comfortable indeed.

"This is certainly a triumph to this entire village, every person has put their share of work into this project and I am very pleased with you all, thank you."

"We must now get started on the school room, which by these standards already shown will not take us very long to complete."

The school room, compared to the house would be very basic, but more than suitable for Africa. It was to be four corner supports and a roof, as in Africa they don't have to worry about keeping warm but must be sure to stay out of the sun and its heat.

The set up for the school room was being discussed as they had previously imagined it to be, but as always Malanda being Malanda had decided to go a different way of doing it.

When they had first discussed it they were working on everything being as simple as they could make and afford, but now Malanda had a slightly different idea.

When they were in Nompulari he had seen a school room and it was just like what the house had been like before they had filled it with furniture.

"Now," he said,

"This beautiful house was built very quickly while most of us were away, look at it."

He turned towards the house and everyone followed what he was looking at.

"Why don't we build a similar building just like the house, we have many hands and we could do it in very good time."

It was agreed and as before Joseph the builder started his pacing to find the right site for the construction.

Never before had this village had a school room and other than the travelling Monks had there ever been a teacher either. This was progression, and it made all the villager's feel good about what they were accomplishing.

As there were children in the village already who could use a teacher, it was decided that they would make enquiries as soon as possible in to how they would get a teacher to live and work in their village. After all, Antonio was now only barely five months old and it would be a while before he required a teacher and the school and the teacher's house would all be completed in a matter of weeks.

Malanda and Tamo would go off together to neighbouring villages and attempt to track down someone working for a Charity and get information from them as to what they now needed to do to get a teacher.

After several days, and several villages, they located a village where members of Oxfam were expected to be calling in the next day or so. They had a simple choice to make, either they would return to their village and return in a day or so and hope that the Oxfam people were there or just stay in that village until they arrived. They decided to stay and wait for them.

The village they were in was only about an hour's walk from their own and when they spoke of what they were doing the Chief there, Mustafa who was of a similar age to Malanda, was also very interested in having their children attend the school, well if the truth were known. It wasn't that Mustafa was interested in having their children educated, but he just didn't want Malanda's village to have something he couldn't have for his children. He would have three boys and two girls who he would want to send to Malanda's village for school.

A deal was struck between the two Chiefs on what Malanda would receive for allowing this, and it turned out to be two bags of maize grain per child per year, the currency of grain, being a normal kind of transaction for these village people.

It was only two days that Malanda and Tamo had to wait for the Oxfam team to arrive and before they had a chance to any other work they had planned, Mustafa called them over to him. He greeted them in his normal tongue to which they replied, but that is where it ended as they were unable to speak any more of the Chief's dialect. Tamo, in his very best broken English explained what they wanted to know and became disheartened when the response from the Oxfam team was they didn't have any idea of how to go about it. However, they were to return to the City after they had finished here and they would ask in their office, someone will know how to go about it. Tamo thanked them on behalf of them all and he and Malanda readied themselves to return to their village.

On their way home they spoke of the great things they as a community had accomplished in recent months and the great things their educated children would accomplish in the years to come. Both men were very pleased with themselves and very proud of the whole village.

For the next few months' life seemed to continue as normally it would in Cobuki. The school room had been completed a good while ago and the teacher's house was now being cleaned regularly even though it as yet didn't have an occupant.

Ammanni had taken the responsibility of this job and was doing it with great pride. Several of the other women had asked if they should do this cleaning job, with Ammanni being the Chiefs' wife, but as not too seem ungrateful, so that she had the perfect excuse to continue, she simply explained that it was Malanda's idea and that nobody else's wife should have the burden of any idea her husband had come up with. The other women took this explanation from Ammanni simply because she was Ammanni, but some also thought that if that was the case they shouldn't have to do any work ever again as everything they did was instigated by Ammanni's husband, but they said nothing as deep down they knew why Ammanni wanted to do the cleaning herself, for the same reason they wanted to do it, they were extremely proud of their school room and teacher's house.

Most of the men from the village that was apart from the fishermen, the very old and of course Malanda had for the last few weeks been out in the fields. It was harvest time and they would be working from dawn to dusk to get all the harvest in. Some men would gather up stalk bails, tie them with another piece of maize straw and leave them were they had been tied.

Others would then collect them and take them to the edge of the field and pass them to the women who would commence in the stripping of the stalks to get all the maize ears from the stalks. Other women would then collect these up and they would be put into what can only be described as great big wooden cauldrons where they would pound them down with a rather large pestle to produce the maize flour.

Having never seen a conveyer belt before, they were doing a grand job at improvising one.

It was during one of these busy days that a Land Rover was seen making its way towards the village. It was still a distance away but clearly on the side of the Land Rover could be seen the logo for Oxfam. It took another five or so minutes for the vehicle to arrive at the village and three people got out, two men and a lady.

In very broken dialect one of the men asked if the Chief was about. Being a bit of a special event for a vehicle to come into the village most of its inhabitants were soon around the vehicle and amongst them of course was Malanda.

"I'm Chief Malanda." Malanda said as he introduced himself.

"Hello Chief, I'm Steve and this is my colleague Owen from Oxfam and we have been given the job of delivering Miss. Rachel Worthington."

Again in a very broken dialect.

"That's nice," said Malanda.

Malanda looked at the lady; a tall and lightly tanned and well dressed and bespectacled lady who was very pleasant to look at who he thought was quite young to be a teacher. Malanda also thought to himself, but why was she here? He'll ask her he thought.

"Why are you here Miss Rachel?" Malanda asked.

In perfect Portuguese, Miss Rachel announced so that all could hear her, that she was their new teacher.

As if they had been rehearsing for this the whole ensemble of the village broke out in a loud cheer and as is their want, some of the villagers started dancing.

Malanda stepped forward in arms reach of Miss Rachel and shock her hand before giving her a very tight hug and must have said 'thank you' a thousand times before he released his grasp of her.

"Miss Rachel will be OK with you now Chief, so if you don't mind, we must be making our way back to the City."

Owen said in much clearer dialect than his friend Steve had spoken.

"Thanks for the lift Steve, have a safe journey back and thanks Owen for giving me the low down on this part of the Country." Rachel said.

The two lads got into their vehicle and with a smoke screen from their exhaust to show where they had been they were off.

"Miss Rachel, thank you for coming to us." Malanda said again and he went to lift her bags for her but wasn't quick enough and two of the villagers had already lifted them and were on their way to the teacher's house.

"This way Miss Rachel, we have a nice house for you."

Malanda said as he led Rachel towards her new house.

As they walked Rachel spotted where the two lads carrying her bags had gone and she said.

"What a lovely house, I'll soon have that as a home that I can enjoy, you shouldn't have gone too so much trouble." Rachel said with a nice smile appearing on her face as she admired what the villagers had done for her arrival.

She was aware that this wasn't the normal house that teachers have to live in as she had been working in Romanbasque for the last two years and had spent that in a circular mud hut.

What she was looking at was perfect and as she entered the house she gasped at what she came across inside.

"How lovely this all is, where did you get it all from?" She asked.

Malanda explained that all will be told later but for now Miss Rachel would need rest after her journey and he hoped she would be very happy with them.

Miss. Rachel thanked Malanda for his kindness and the house emptied and she was for the first time alone in her new home.

She wondered as she walked around investigating her new home, how they got all the stuff it's beautiful and so far away from anywhere where they could have bought it without difficulty.

It wasn't long before she decided to take the Chief's advice and she removed her shoes and settled down on the bed for a rest. She had been travelling for fifteen hours to get to the village and had started out the evening before. She had tried to sleep while they travelled but could hardly get a wink in the back of the Land Rover as it bumped its way over the bush. Steve wasn't the best at avoiding the pot holes in the make shift roads either and she had been given a bump on her head more than once during the trip.

She settled down thinking of the welcome she had been given when she arrived and thought she would be happy here, nice people, and as she was thinking, she fell into a deep sleep.

6

It was the next morning when Rachel's door opened and she walked out into the sunshine. At first she couldn't see anyone about, but as she stepped on to her path of stones there was Ammanni.

"Hello Miss Rachel I'm Ammanni." Ammanni said in way of introduction.

"Hello Ammanni, I'm Rachel." Rachel replied.

"I know Miss Rachel and we are so glad to have you here with us, may I clean your house now?" she asked.

"No, I'll be fine thanks." Rachel said,

But as she was saying it Ammanni passed her and had started to clean about the house before Rachel had time to finish her sentence.

Rachel looked at her watch and saw that it was already nine o'clock and realised that Ammanni would have probably been waiting outside the house since dawn to do the cleaning. Rachel called inside to Ammanni.

"See you later." and left her to get on with her cleaning.

Rachel walked off around the village and she could see in the distance Malanda looking out to the fields and watching his men working on the harvest.

The fields looked fairly bare to Rachel and she took it that the harvest was very nearly over. To one side of the field she saw the women working on the maize and made her way towards them.

Only a few steps into her walk and she was noticed by Malanda.

"Miss Rachel, Miss Rachel, is you well after your sleep?"

Malanda shouted as he made his way towards her.

"Fine thank you, I had a wonderful sleep."

"Is there anything you need, we will have it put right for you?"

"No, thank you Chief, everything is fine and I certainly didn't expect such a fine house to live in."

"We wanted everything to be right for you; we are hoping you will want to stay with us." Malanda said.

"If everything is like you treated me so far I would love to stay." Rachel said.

"Can I see the school room please?" Rachel asked.

"This way please, I'll take you there." Malanda said as he led the way to the school room.

The school room was just behind Rachel's house but at the back of it so she had walked away from it when she left her house.

They arrived at the school room and Rachel said

"You have done a great job here Chief, you should be very proud of it."

"We are but you must let us know if we need anything else and we will get it for you." Malanda said.

Rachel looked around at the desks, the chairs, her desk and what must be a black board but in fact was just an old piece of tin which had been surrounded by a frame of wood.

"I'm sure we will all be very comfortable here Chief, have we got paper and pencils for the students?" Rachel asked.

"I have brought what I could with me but there is not that much." Rachel added.

"I will get someone off to the City when we are ready to deliver some of the harvest and they can bring some back with them." Malanda said.

"We will do fine I have enough for now." Rachel said.

Rachel continued to look around and was very impressed in all that she saw,

"What a great place to have to work, it's lovely, thank you for asking me to come." Rachel said.

"But we didn't ask you." Malanda said.

"What!" Rachel responded.

"The first we knew of you coming here was when you arrived. I did ask someone from Oxfam to find out how we went about getting a teacher to come to our village, but that was weeks ago and we haven't heard anything since then." Malanda said

Hoping this wouldn't change Rachel's mind and she would leave.

"I have known I was coming here for about four weeks but first had to wait for a replacement to arrive before I could leave my other school." Rachel said.

"Not to worry, I'm here now and from what I have seen so far very happy to be here." Rachel added.

Malanda smiled and inwardly had a great big sigh of relief. They had all worked so hard to get everything ready and to lose their teacher before she had even started to teach would be terrible. He was happy Miss Rachel was happy and he was sure that everyone in the village would all do their best to ensure Rachel remained happy. He had only just met Rachel but already he liked her and hoped that she liked being with them for a long time to come.

Rachel asked how many students she would have and Malanda

explained that for now she would have just three from this village and possibly up to five from a neighbouring village. Rachel seemed pleased with the number of children and hoped that it would be more as time went on.

"And of course, you will be joining us from time to time?" Rachel asked.

"Me!" said Malanda.

"I am too old for this new education." Malanda said quite embarrassed.

"We will see." Added Rachel and left it like that.

Malanda excused himself saying he had to go to the fields to see what was happening with the harvest, but Rachel knew the real reason, she had embarrassed him and for now she wouldn't mention it again until she felt the time was right to tackle him about it.

Rachel hoped that she could start classes for all ages as she had been very successful in her last village, and many of the villagers had joined in the classes. She knew she was here for the children in the main but was sure she could bring an even better benefit to the village by educating as many of the villagers as she was able.

Rachel returned to her house to get some things she needed to put in the school room and she found Ammanni still there working.

"You have done a lovely job, everything is so nice, and I think I am really going to enjoy it here." Rachel said.

"I do hope so; my husband has worked so hard to get everything just right for you." Ammanni said.

"Who is your husband Ammanni?" Rachel asked.

"Chief Malanda is my husband you have been talking to him." Ammanni said.

Rachel found it strange that the Chief's wife was doing the cleaning in her home but said nothing. What Rachel needed now was a shower and asked Ammanni where it the shower block was situated.

"Shower block." Ammanni said.

"Yes, where we can get a wash." Rachel said.

"Shower block, I don't think we have one of them." Ammanni said.

"Not to worry I will go down to the river for a wash." Rachel said and got her things and made her way off towards the river.

Ammanni took flight and ran off to find her husband in a bit of a state if you ask me.

"Malanda, Malanda she wants a shower block." Ammanni shouted as she ran towards her husband.

"A shower block? What is a shower block?" Malanda asked.

"I don't know but she wants one, what are we going to do. It has something to do with cleaning." Ammanni said.

Malanda took flight to find Rachel and found her at the river in a most uncovered state of dress. Rachel dropped beneath the water line so that Malanda couldn't get a view of her fairly large breasts. Malanda neared and just said.

"What is a shower block we will have one as soon as you tell us what one is and where to get one from."

He shouted, as by this time Rachel had made her way out into the water and was about ten metres away from the shore.

"Come in Miss Rachel." Malanda shouted to her.

"I'm OK here; I'll wait until you go before I come in." Rachel said.

"Please come in, you are out where the crocodiles will know you are there." Malanda shouted back to Rachel.

Rachel didn't need telling twice and was urgently making her way nearer the shore as fast as she could. Her bare breasts were the last thing on her mind as she reached the shore and ran out into Malanda's safe arms.

Malanda, either the courteous gent or even possibly the fact that this was the first time he had seen a naked white woman, quickly covered her up with the towel she had left on the shore, but continued to hold her tight until she had completely calmed down. She may have been a white woman but that experience certainly took the little colour she had out of her.

Rachel dressed and with Malanda by her side as if for protection made her way back up to the village. As they walked Malanda asked again about what the shower block was and where they could get one.

It just happened that when Rachel was at the other village a team from Charity working there installed a shower block and Rachel had watched how it had been constructed and would be able to show this village how to construct their own.

When they returned to the village Rachel armed herself with some paper and a pencil and set out to explain to Malanda exactly how they could do it for themselves.

Now even though Malanda was the great Chief of his people he became totally confused as Rachel drew various drawings to help her explanation.

"Hang on a minute, Miss. Rachel, I'll get Brother Joseph to come over, he will understand what you are saying."

Brother Joseph joined them and again Rachel explained what she had seen built at her other village and Joseph understood completely, she thought.

That afternoon Joseph gathered a couple of men to help him and began the work in earnest to get it finished for Miss. Rachel to use the following day.

The shower block frame went up without a problem, with reeds being used to lash small saplings together to form screen walls. A roof was constructed in the same way and that was added, then a hollowed out tree was placed on top of the roof to act as the water tank. No problems so far. Barks were removed from trees to form a water channel and they were directed into where the person would stand to have a shower, even a make shift pulley system was made to use as an on/off switch for the flow of water, still no problems. Then the water tank had to be filled up to complete the operation. Well, just think a litre of water actually weighs one kilo, the hollowed out tree, which would act as the water tank held approximately thirty litres, which is thirty kilo's in weight, plus the weight of the hollowed out tree, equalled, calamity! The whole roof structure; after commencing with a creek, which became louder for a moment, was the cue for the tree and all the water to fall straight through and crash to the floor. Plan 'B' was quickly brought into play and the shower block was finished, this time, safe to use. It was a strange pylon of reed tied trees that eventually held up the water tank, but it worked.

Rachel had already started to have an effect on her new friends but this was real advancement for a distant village in Northern Romanbasque and the villager's liked it. They liked Rachel as well, for as she walked around the village she was always full of smiles and happy to stop and talk with anyone who wanted to talk with her.

She had now been in the village for only a day or so but went to Malanda and told him that she would like to start teaching in a day or so if that was alright with him. He agreed and said he would send a messenger to the adjacent village to inform the Chief there of the plans.

The day before teaching would start it was Sunday and at the weekly service many prayers were said for Rachel and the school and thanks were given to God for sending Rachel to them.

What everyone in the village had set out to achieve was now ready. They had their school room, they had their teacher who had very quickly became a very good friend to all of them, and now their next step to educated their children, could begin.

The first day of school began and Rachel was very pleased that she had five children who attended the lessons.

This was a new challenge for Rachel but a huge step forward for the people of Cobuki, so much so that the children attended inside the school room but most of the available villager's watched on through the windows, cheering at points in the lesson that Rachel for one couldn't really understand why they had.

The obvious first lesson was the ABC, which Rachel would write on the board and mouth the sounds, instead of just five children answering her teachings she had approximately forty adults outside joining in as well.

The excitement continued throughout the day and at the end of lessons a tumultuous applause rang out for the new teacher. Rachel replied by applauding all their efforts.

Over the next few days the hangers on got less and less until on the fifth day Rachel was teaching just the class members who by then had nicely increased to seven. Six children and Ammanni whom her husband had suggested would be a good idea for her to join in.

The school room was going fine and the children were not just enjoying their new education but a result from the teaching was being realised when it was observed that they were actually learning from their Miss. Rachel and retaining it.

* * * *

Rachel was soon going to reach her two years at Cobuki and that would mean her contract would come to an end. However, she loved her job and more to the point she loved her new people. She penned a letter and it was despatched to Nompulari where the Charity that controlled the teachers in Romanbasque had their Headquarters. It only took about three weeks and a reply arrived with the same runner who had delivered her letter.

Schools for Villages
In Common Goals

Dear Miss. Worthington

Subject: Extension of assignment.

Further to your recent request for an extension of tour within the village of Cobuki, it is hereby granted for a period only to be determined by your wishes.

Please contact us when you wish to be re-assigned or have any further wishes to which we can be of assistance.

Yours sincerely,

David Beasley

Area Director

After reading her letter Rachel turned to Malanda who was waiting with baited breath to find out its contents and said;

"It's OK I can stay as long as I want, and as long as you will have me."

Malanda was overjoyed and made his feelings audibly known

to all within his hearing, running around the village announcing this great news.

Malanda was overjoyed with the news but Rachel was also pleased with the way in which the Director had worded the letter.

"Further wishes to which we can be of assistance." She read again to herself.

She decided to write back to the Director and ask for more supplies that had been turning up and to possibly get an additional teacher. For in just the two years she had been there, her school attendances had increased from the initial five children to that of fifteen children during the day and some twenty odd adults she was teaching during the evenings.

After just two months from writing her second letter, she received a reply in the form of a Miss. Celia Brown. Celia Brown had just completed her studies as a teacher but had decided that a full break from the 'Hubbub' of City life is what she needed to do. She had signed up for a one year 'Sabbatical' contract and had been offered Romanbasque.

Rachel and Celia together looked like Mother and Daughter as Rachel now in her fifth year in Africa had somewhat aged to look a good deal older than her 28 years, and Celia coming straight from England at the mere age of 21 years old looked considerably younger for her age. However, the pair hit it off within moments of their first meeting. Rachel a veteran of Africa and Celia a Novice from Barnsley who's furthest travels to date had been the Algarve in Portugal.

When Celia's sabbatical was over she was immediately replaced by Mary Tyler from Birmingham and she was further replaced by Ken Bright from Stevenage.

Ken's replacement was Geri Armchurch who was another student direct from training who came from Sheffield via Oxford

University and she would prove to have an overwhelming influence on the young Antonio who was just about to start his studies.

Antonio now five years old was due to start school in just two days and his father wanted it to be a special day for him but also for the village. His thoughts were that it was Antonio's birth that started all this and it should be celebrated.

Malanda spoke to some of the Elders and they didn't have a problem with there being a celebration, there again, the Elders didn't have a problem having a celebration for any occasion, so the fact that this celebration would have some rhyme reason and substance was a good thing.

Along with Antonio, there would be another two children starting the school on the same day. It was arranged that all three sets of parents would honour their children by this celebration and that it would happen that evening.

Within any Province, City, Town or even small village in Africa it doesn't take long to organise a party and everyone would do their bit to make it happen. Women started preparing food; no more food than they would normally prepare for their own families but when put all together with everybody else's it would look like a feast to behold.

The men of the village organised lanterns in an area where the party would happen and fallen trees were positioned to allow for suitable seating for all.

The party started just after dusk and the children who would attend the school room were shown around the other villager's, a speech was given by all the proud fathers and the mothers cried. Not that different from here to good old Blighty.

After only the first hour and a half the three children along with all the others under the age of about ten were shuffled off to their beds but the party continued long into the night, none of the men, after a great deal to drink were in a position by then to know why there had been a party in the first place, but they enjoyed it all the same.

7

Antonio's first day of school arrived and it began with a procession from his hut with his father and mother beside him. He lived only twenty metres from the school but his father decided that a journey around the village would be the best way to mark his first day of education. As they made their way around the village cheers broke out, applause from some was given and as they neared the school room entrance there was a formation befitting any good guard of honour to welcome Antonio into his school.

Antonio was met by Miss. Rachel and Miss. Geri and after some convincing he was allowed into the school room with his parents remaining outside.

Many people remained for a while outside the school room but Malanda was still there when they took a break some two hours later.

He stayed to watch the children play and he walked towards Antonio to speak to him but was interrupted by Rachel.

"Chief, leave him with us now, it will be better for him."

Malanda didn't answer but just turned on his heels and was gone. For the next few days he could be seen trying to watch his son at his studies but the well adjusted shutters of the windows as Rachel notice him soon made it clear to him that this had to stop.

Antonio liked Miss. Rachel a lot and had now known her for

most of his life but he really took a liking to Miss. Geri. Miss. Geri would talk to Antonio about what she had done through her studies and explained to him how far he could go if he really applied himself to his studies. Antonio now only five year old listened very carefully to what Miss. Geri had to say and it really had an influence on him, even at this early age.

I would expect that from the first time he could understand anything his father Malanda had been briefing him on the great things he would be expected to achieve and now he was hearing it from someone else.

During his studies Antonio was very intent and was a good student. His work was done at a high standard even from the start and as he aged he improved to the point that he was leading the other students in the class. It became obvious that he was bound for greater things and he would definitely be a good candidate for University as his father had predicted on the day of his birth.

Miss. Rachel had remained at the village and was now prepared to stay until Antonio was ready to leave this school. Miss. Geri had left the village and a further seven replacements had been to teach at the school but what Miss. Geri had told Antonio in that first year of his schooling had stuck and he was out to achieve it.

Antonio, now thirteen years of age was getting close to taking the Bursary exam, where if he passed it would allow him free entrance into a good University at the age of seventeen after attending a school in the City for the next three years to enable him to sit the GCSE equivalent exams.

For many hours at night Antonio would study his work and each morning he would have a list of questions for Miss. Rachel to answer or clarify for him. He was such an avid student that he came up with a few questions that caught Miss. Rachel out, and she was the person who had taught him in the first place.

As his exam neared Antonio would spend more and more time studying and being assisted by Miss. Rachel. He would ask questions, Miss Rachel would answer them and then Antonio would question the answer. From this Rachel new that Antonio would be a very good student not only at the Bursary school but also for further education.

The exam papers arrived by Land Rover and it was Antonio and Claris that would be taking this year's exams. They sat apart in a quite school room and on the instruction of the monitoring teacher commenced their exams. Claris started writing almost immediately but Antonio just sat and read the paper. As was his want, Malanda was watching through the window from a distance so not to disturb the children or to have been told off by the monitor, but something was wrong. Malanda made his way quickly over to where Rachel was standing and informed her that his son wasn't doing anything and demanded to know why.

"It's OK Chief, Antonio has his own way of doing things and one thing he always does is read everything and work out the best way to attack the problem, he will be fine, trust me."

Malanda wasn't very happy with her answer but thought better of questioning her as he knew she was normally right.

He walked back to his peering point and his son was still just sat there reading. Malanda was still worried but stood in silence worrying about his son and then; Antonio picked up his pen and started to answer the paper. He wrote and wrote and never seemed to take a break at all and was finished well before the time allowed was up.

"How did you do son?" Malanda asked Antonio.

"It was OK but they will have to be clearer on a few points, which I have written at the side of the paper for them." Antonio said.

Malanda not really knowing what his son was talking about left in a bit of a state thinking his son may have failed the exam.

Antonio had many discussions with Rachel over the exam paper and it was during one of these discussions that a vehicle approached the village. They stopped their talks and went to see who it was.

When the vehicle came to a stop a large burly man stepped out and immediately recognised Rachel. Not because he knew her but knew that she was the only white women in this village. He walked over to her and asked,

"Miss. Worthington?"

"Yes, and you are?"

"Pete Graham, Headmaster of the Bursary school Nompulari and I'm looking for an Antonio Thica."

"I'm Antonio Thica how can I help you?" Antonio answered in his near perfect English.

"Sir, I have come to invite you to join my school." Pete said.

"Your exam results were excellent and I would like you to come back with me now if you are able," invited Pete.

As they spoke, Malanda arrived and Rachel explained who Mr. Graham was and why he was here.

Malanda stretched out his hand to welcome Mr. Graham and took him to the school room to show him where Antonio had been taught. He told him of how Miss. Rachel had taught his son and the wonderful things she had done since she had been with them. He basically went on and on and on, but for a while, nobody was prepared to stop him.

It was Pete Graham who eventually brought Malanda's oration to a close when he asked Malanda if he would like to know why his son had been selected.

"Oh yes Mr. Pete, please tell us why."

"Well it just so happens that your son Antonio has achieved number one for these exams in the country and you should be very proud of him." Pete said.

Malanda's face bore a wide smile and he turned to Antonio and hugged him, telling him of the pride he had always had for his son and he knew he was destined for so much more than he had ever achieved.

"So what happens now Mr. Pete?"

"Well if you will permit me, I would like to take Antonio back with me so he can start as soon as possible into the new term."

"That is not a problem." Malanda said.

"Is it Antonio?" Malanda directed to his son.

"I am ready father and if Mr. Pete can give me a while to pack some things I am happy to go with him." Antonio said.

"Right, that's just fine. You go and pack young man and I will talk to your father." Pete said.

When Antonio disappeared to pack his bag for the journey, which wouldn't be that much, but he would be taking some of his books with him, Pete explained to Malanda exactly what would happen from now on.

'Your son has won a full Bursary at the school, which means this will cost you nothing for him to attend, but this will only be for the Bursary school. You might like to take heed that from his current standard we will more than expect Antonio to go on to further education which could have a price on it.'

However, this would not be for another three years so Malanda did have time to save for the future.

Pete also added 'that once he had had time to personally assess Antonio he would write to Miss. Rachel and explain further what the costs might be expected to be for Antonio to continue with his studies after the Bursary school.'

Malanda actually understood little of what Pete was saying for at that moment his head was in the clouds with the utmost pride for his son. Later Rachel would have to explain all that was said, for now only thoughts of his son were occupying his mind.

Antonio returned with his mother, who as normal was crying and wishing her son well. He had just a small pack of things with which he was about to embark on a three year study course many kilometres away from home. That was, and still is quite normal for an African child. They don't really pack what they need; they pack all that they own.

Final goodbyes and good lucks were passed around and soon the vehicle containing Pete and Antonio was driving off into the bush to start the new life for Antonio that his father had always worked towards. A proud day for Malanda and his entire villager's as he realised that without their help and support this day might never have come.

At the start of his studies at his new school Antonio settled in well, making friends with others his age and with most of the teachers. This continued for his complete course of study and during his time at the school he only returned home on just four occasions and on the fourth time it was at the end of the three years.

He had, as expected worked very hard during his time there and he had, again as expected, won a good Bursary to move on to further education. First, he would have to attend another school in Nompulari for a two year period to enable him to gain his equivalent of 'A' levels, but he had already been given, on the outcome of these further exams an opportunity to go on to a University in Britain.

All the people of the village welcomed him back as if they all knew he was going to be the man they all thought he would be back when they made the decision to build their school room many years before. When they had given their backing to Malanda's idea, and when they had also taken the decision that this would cost them from that point and for a long time after Antonio had finished his studies, but they all wanted this, not just for Antonio. It was for their children's futures, the future of the people of the village, and they were prepared for it.

Over the many years, money, even though just small amounts, had been saved for this very purpose and their joint goal of having a child from their village become fully educated in order to move the village forward.

Antonio would only stay home on this occasion for a two week period. He had an eight week break but had volunteered to work with a Charity for this time.

For the time he did spend at home very few people would see him as he would be working, reading through his books to gain even more knowledge for his task ahead of him.

After this short visit home he was collected by members of the Charity and that would be the last anyone of the village would see of him for the next two years. Of course he would have been given time off but his studies were more important to him than visits home so he would remain in Nompulari, sometimes all alone at the school and read and learn and better himself as much as he could. Antonio enjoyed learning and he knew he must one day be able to repay his fellow villager's for all their hard work and backing for him to be able to do this, not just for him, but for them.

Depending on the results from his exams he had been offered a place at the University of Bradford, England to study a course on Community and Environmental Regeneration and up to now there was no reason why he shouldn't achieve this place, but he would not be taking the chance of failing to gain this place, so he would study at every opportunity he would have.

Due to his dedication to learn he was in good favour with most of the teachers at his school and they would spend long hours discussing with him the many questions he would have from reading his books. Antonio would question everything to find out what he wanted to know and he would want to know where other people had gone wrong in the past. He would not be putting himself in a position of possible failure. He would be the best and give to his village and even in time his country the best that he could to move them forward, and for this he needed the knowledge, all the knowledge that he could get and from anyone who was prepared to give it to him.

Antonio's exams at this level would have the same outcome as always, and he passed with flying colours and had no problem gaining the place at the University of Bradford he so much desired.

He would take up the place in September, which was nearly six months away so he returned to his village for a long deserved holiday with his family, for once he went off to England he would not be able to return for the duration of the course, however long it would take for holiday flight money would not be available for any returns home for holidays.

During his time home he sat for many hours with his father Malanda and would give informed educational talks to him, most of which was far too much for Malanda to comprehend, but he still listened intently to his son who now he not only loved but admired for all the hard work he done and for what he had accomplished so far.

Antonio would need to leave the village at least a month before his flight to England as he had a three thousand mile journey to the airport to overcome before the flight, so Malanda arranged a party to ensure his son would first have a good send off.

The day of the party given in his honour arrived and everybody from a distance around had come to see him off and to wish him well on his adventures.

During the evening he had been garlanded in flowers by the young girls of the village, given presents by the mothers, fathers and extended family members, few of which would prove very useful on his travels but he accepted them graciously and said he would do his very best for them all.

The party continued late into the night and continued into early the next morning and it was a great celebration not only for Antonio but the villager's felt that they had also achieved great things even though they had all had to make many sacrifices to get their man this far, but they were pleased they had made the sacrifices as they could see that it was now starting to pay off.

It was as the sun was starting to rise that Antonio and his father said their final farewells to the last of their guests and made their way off to have some well earned sleep.

On the day of departure, all the village lined up to wish him well and wave him off as he started on the 3,000 kilometre bus ride to the City where he would board a plane for his new life.

8

Antonio was born and raised in a village known as Cobuki on the banks of Lake Ryasari in Northern Romanbasque. Cobuki was a small village from which the village's main industries were farming the land and fishing the waters of Lake Ryasari which shared its shores with the Countries of Malawi and Tanzania.

Now it was time for him to leave and travel great distances, which he had never encountered before in his life. His journey would commence on foot for the first three days until he reached a village that was served by bus.

Even the bus ride would bring new experiences into Antonio's what now began to become apparent very sheltered life. He had gained a great deal more of life's experiences than most in his village by spending such a long time in Nompulari, but very little compared to what he would experience from now on. He began to realise this was the first time he had ever travelled South for any distance. He was experiencing flora and fauna which he had never came across before. The colours of the peoples' dress in the villages he passed through were also new to him, but the biggest difference he was experiencing is that the people were much lighter in skin colour that to his.

Antonio had come from a village in the very North of Romanbasque where he lived very close to the Equator. Now he was travelling south towards Romanbasqui, Romanbasque's capital City where he would board a plane to leave Romanbasque for the very first time.

Romanbasqui is still an equatorial area but is situated below the Tropic of Capricorn so the climate is somewhat different from the village in which Antonio was raised. For the first time in his life he was feeling a bit chilly in the daytime, and this was definitely a new experience for him.

The bus ride had taken 14 days to reach Romanbasqui due to it being just after the rainy season and the roads were full with potholes that had to be carefully negotiated by the driver. At times the passengers would have to disembark to allow for the vehicle to be able to make the manoeuvre around what could be described in the western world as craters, but for the Romanbasque's these could only be described as normal road conditions on most of the highways.

Even leaving the bus for this reason caused Antonio to have yet another experience he wasn't quite used too and thought he would never be able to continue at times. The reason was that when he had first started out on this epic journey he was among just four other passengers, which was normal from the village to one of the nearby towns. As the journey progressed more and more passengers joined the trip. At first Antonio had had a seat and was able to look around and generally be very comfortable on his ride. Now he had been joined by some thirty other passengers all travelling in what could only be described as a not too trustworthy, aged Volkswagen transit van. When he had to leave the bus it was a race if he wanted to stand any chance of regaining a seat to continue the journey. Sometimes he would, sometimes he wouldn't get a seat but he soon came to realise that either way he was in between the devil and the deep blue sea. If he regained a seat he was stuck inside the bus, crammed to the gunnels with sweaty bodies all around him all jostling for a piece of comfort which had not actually been there from the start. If he didn't get a seat he would have to hang on the outside of the bus and stand on the runners. Not too bad you say, and this would be cool and the pace of the bus wasn't that fast anyway. However, we are talking Africa in the baking sun where flies and insects would be looking for a comfortable ride themselves. Each stop after this situation would cause Antonio to need to thoroughly clean himself down from the insects that had adhered themselves to him during the previous leg of the journey.

As he entered Romanbasqui for a short time Antonio experienced what was to be his first time on what could only be said as being a proper road. The smooth tarmac on which he was now travelling was such a contrast to what he had been travelling on.

His first encounter with tall buildings was also something which he became very nervous of seeing. All around him great towers of buildings made him look constantly upwards. If only he knew what was to come as he moved further afield and out his native homeland.

The bus stopped in the centre of the city which meant he now had to find his way to the Airport. He asked about and soon he was on another bus, or Volkswagen van towards the airport. He was now travelling on concrete roads which added a great many bumps to his ride.

Soon the Airport came into view. Romanbasqui International Airport the sign said and this was an anxious time for Antonio for the last stage of his travel within his own country had come to an end. He was now destined for the big outside world overseas, other cultures and other experiences he would never have thought possible a few months earlier.

At the airport porters came to the bus to hopefully carry someone's bags and be rewarded by a few Reticalie for their efforts. Antonio's bags consisted of a blanket like wrap which contained one change of formal African dress and a book given to him by his teacher at school. Other than that, he had the clothes which he stood up in, his passport, which by now was fairly thumbed from being looked at by all the people of the village, his flight ticket and $200 which was the total that the village people were able to amass to start him on way. Still the porters tried to assist Antonio but he knew that he would have to be very careful with his money so he politely declined their assistance.

The Government had assisted with the school fees for Antonio by paying the most part of them. The village however, would have to repay a total of $1,000 over the next four years as their part in sending their scholar away to University. Not a lot of money for a whole village, but that calculates that each villager may only earn around $30 a year it becomes a feat in itself.

As Antonio entered the airport he was able to recognise some of the businesses that he had also seen in Nompulari; the shoe shine boys, the water boys and of course the beggars trying to amass a few Reticalie for a little food at the end of their day.

The one thing that did unnerve him quite a bit was the amount of people. All in one place, some dashing some just standing around, families, couples and loners just like him.

He made his way through the crowds and was stopped by one of the customs officials to search his wrap. He opened it up showing the contents of just his formal African wear and was quickly ushered on. Next to the ticket counter where he would book in his wrap, being his only baggage and was issued his boarding card, then told to go to the tax counter,

"Tax counter?" enquired Antonio.

"Yes the flight tax of 36,000 Reticalie has to be paid over there before you can go through to the departure lounge." Instructed the ticket checker.

Antonio made way over to the tax counter and duly paid his 36,000 Reticalie for the privilege of being given a stamp on the back of his boarding card to allow him to enter the departure lounge.

It's difficult to work this tax out. It doesn't matter to where you are flying, everybody has to pay, who is getting this money? The normal flight taxes are part of the purchase of your ticket but in Africa something's are a little different, to say the least and I suppose the least said the better in most cases.

Now, here is another case where you shouldn't really say anything because it doesn't get you anywhere if you do.

Antonio had paid his 36,000 Reticalie from his $200 which would have been approximately $2.18, to do this he handed over a $5 bill, which would have left him with $2.82 but the change is given in the local currency, which of course is Reticalie. This worked out at 4,794 Reticalie, which when he arrived at the departure lounge was confiscated from him as you are not allowed to take any Reticalie out of Romanbasque. Consequently, the cost of his flight tax had now added up to $5. $2.18 for the tax and $2.82 for the policeman on the gate of the departure lounge, no receipt, you just have to hand it over. As I have said, least said the better.

After going through the search area, Antonio entered the International Departure Lounge of the airport. A scant place approximately thirty metres long and ten metres wide with shops at one end of it. Antonio had some time to wait so decided to have a look in the shops. He looked but at no time thought of possibly purchasing anything. Romanbasque's can rarely afford such things that these shops sell and really wouldn't find a use for them even if they bought something. The shops sold such items as jewellery, crystal, perfumes, leather bags and purses and of course the customary duty free shop for cigarettes and alcohol. Antonio looked, but didn't buy anything not just that he didn't need anything but he wouldn't have had enough money even he wanted something. You get the idea, the typical airport shop, overpriced goods that you really don't need anyway, especially when you are going on a trip.

So, with just $195 of his original $200 left in his pocket, Antonio took a seat and waited for the call to join his plane.

It was a good hour later that the call came for passengers on the flight to Johannesburg to make their way to the lounge door. Antonio stood up and immediately found himself in a queue. As is normally the case at Romanbasqui airport the only people in the departure lounge are all catching the same plane as international flights are very few and far between.

As he stood and slowly shuttled forward he could hear one of the policemen shouting that all passports and boarding cards are to be ready for inspection. He had his out and ready ever since entering the lounge, gripping them firmly for one reason for their security and the other, thought's of his first aeroplane flight were making him very uneasy but excited all at the same time.

The queue moved slowly forward and he could now see the huge plane he would be joining looming on the apron about one hundred metres from where he was standing. As he moved through the door he was asked to identify his luggage, which he did and it was added to the trolley which would take it to the plane.

The walk to the plane made Antonio more anxious as he realised that the loud drone was in fact coming from the plane he would be boarding. At the bottom of the stairs he stopped, which caused a shuffle behind him but was also noticed by the stewardess who was stood at the top of the stairs. She came down to Antonio, held his hand and said,

"Afternoon Sir, welcome aboard, would you like to follow me?"

This gave Antonio the boost he needed and he followed the stewardess up the stairs and on to the plane.

"Can I see your boarding card please Sir?" asked the stewardess.

Antonio showed the boarding card and the stewardess led the way to his seat.

"The seat by the window is your seat Sir, and I'll be back shortly to see if everything is alright."

"Thank you." Antonio said as they parted company and Antonio made his way through the other seats to reach his.

Antonio sat down in his seat and immediately noticed the broacher in front of him that stated 'Please Read'. So he opened it and began to read and digest all of its information. He had read it three times when the stewardess returned to ask if he had settled in.

"Nothing to worry about Sir, we do this all the time." The stewardess said.

"I realise that but it is my first time and it's a bit strange to me." Antonio said.

The stewardess in a state of busy nodded and walked away down towards the back of the plane.

"If you need anything Sir, just ring the bell above your head and one of us will come to you." The stewardess's words fading as she distanced herself from Antonio.

Antonio looked out of the window on to the apron where he could see the baggage handlers loading the side of the plane. So much luggage as he thought and wondered if they would get it all on or would they leave some there for the next plane to take. Or would they just leave it for when someone came back to Romanbasqui to collect it.

The doors were eventually closed and the Captain's voice welcomed all the passengers onboard. He explained the flight would take approximately one hour to reach Johannesburg and that he anticipated that they would arrive as scheduled. The cabin staff then took over and explained the safety drills. Antonio did wonder how the drop would be if he had to use a safety door at 28,000 ft.

The plane slowly edged forward and they made their way to the runway. They were to take off on the North runway so they had to taxi for a far distance before they reached the point where they would start their take off from.

The engines roared and slowly the plane lurched forward, just at the same time that Antonio's stomach decided to do the same and he could feel the little food he had eaten trying to make its way up towards his throat. He gulped as the plane started its acceleration and the food went back to whence it came and moments later they were airborne.

The excitement took over from Antonio's fears and he looked out the window to watch the ground getting further and further away, the buildings becoming smaller and at that moment he felt good, he felt very good and his new life in England was becoming a reality at last. He had done what was asked of him and now he was being rewarded with the trip of a life time.

During the flight Antonio was served with a light meal as it had been described over the speaker system by the head stewardess, but for him it was plenty. He ate the cheese roll and packed the cake and apple into one of the many sick bags in the front of the seat to eat later. A few minutes after the cabin staff had collected all the lunch packaging Antonio felt the plane start to go down and looking out of the window he could start to see for the first time the outline of the Metropolitan City of Johannesburg. He would very soon be in another country for the first time in his life and his excitement was overwhelming and he was looking forward to it.

With a bump the plane landed and the Captain once again spoke to the passengers, thanking them for travelling with South African Airways and hoped they would soon come back and fly with them again. The outside temperature was 16oC and a nice clear day the Captain told them but when the cabins doors were opened again Antonio felt a bit chilly. 16oC, that's a nice warm temperature but not for people who come from near the equator. Antonio had never seen a thermometer but he knew that compared with home this was cold. Within the Village of

Cobuki, not that they have ever measured it they would not have ever experienced a temperature of less than 22oC and that would be if it had been measured in the dead of night. Even their rainy days would be warm and certainly 16oC would not have ever been experienced by Antonio.

He left the plane and joined the awaiting bus as quickly as he could but the bus also caught him unawares, as he had never seen such a nice looking vehicle. Wide seats on all sides greeted him and the engine purred instead of the normal labour of the Volkswagen Transit Vans he was used to riding in. When full the bus moved off quietly and smoothly and Antonio found he was appreciating the comfort he was experiencing.

The bus came to halt outside the terminal building and without anyone saying anything the people started to move off the bus into a queue entering the passport control. Through a corridor, up a stair and he was in what he could only describe as the biggest shop he had ever seen.

The terminal building of Johannesburg Airport is huge to say the least. Antonio entered the building with his eyes getting larger and larger as he tried to take in as much of this sight as he could. He looked at everything he could in the time he had to spare, which was as he had been told, four hours to look over this great place and discover what was on offer. He spent time in the electronics' shop where he watched television for a good hour, just stood there watching. They did have television in Nompulari but not where he could watch it regularly. He looked over the computers, which he had used but not like these, the latest on the market with all the up to date systems. He was amazed at what he could see and what he could buy if only he had the money. The Modern World was really starting to have an effect on Antonio, and he liked it.

He entered a shop selling African Souvenirs, which consisted of carvings that many people in his own village would do when they had spare time and give them to the children to play with.

These carvings were for sale at what Antonio could only say, were a fortune.

Disappointed over the costs of these trinkets he made his way over to a seating area where he could sit and digest what he had seen so far. He was nicely digesting when he heard the call for his flight and that he would now have to go to 'Gate 37.' He picked up his sick bag of food supplies and checked out which way he was to go. He looked up at all the numbers, found the way he had to go and made his way towards the gate. Half an hour later he was still walking but could see the gate number and again he joined on to a long queue. He was starting to realise that the Modern World has lots of things that he definitely didn't know of or had experienced much of in Northern Romanbasque, and that were queues.

He showed his passport and boarding card and joined another bus to take them to the plane, which pleased him no end. He liked these buses and was a bit disappointed when the ride took less than five minutes to reach the plane.

Expecting the same size plane that he had travelled from Romanbasque on, he was taken aback when he saw the Boeing 747 stood awaiting their arrival. This monster of a plane was something Antonio just didn't expect to see waiting for him. Again his fears and anticipation rejoined him as he ascended the stairs to the cabin. He was met with the same courteous greeting from one of the cabin staff and shown to his seat situated over the wing again next to the window. He looked out of the window and down to the ground and realised just how high he in fact was from the ground. He looked forward down the plane and it seemed to go on forever, and all these people, how would we ever get off the ground? He thought to himself.

He was surprised when the plane started to move so soon after he had joined it. They taxied for what seemed like an age before turning to the runway and as soon as they were straight, acceleration ripped through the plane and expecting a short run along the runway as when they took off from Romanbasqui, Antonio once again got a bit nervy when the plane took for what he thought for ever trying to take off and he thought the plane just wasn't going to make it, when, suddenly, the plane lifted gently off the runway and into the air.

9

The plane soared upwards at an oblique angle for what seemed like an age to Antonio, but eventually after about twenty minutes it levelled out and Antonio felt a bit easier and was able to relax his grip from the seat arms he had held so tightly for all of this time. Ping, was heard through the cabin and the stewardesses started to move around the plane. Antonio felt a bit better knowing that the professionals were now happy enough to move around and he took a last look out through the window to see the view, which was now unfortunately blocked by the clouds.

A few minutes passed with Antonio looking around the plane at the mass of people that he hadn't really noticed before now, as his head at been facing the window ever since he had boarded the plane with him taking in all the new experiences he could of international flight. He looked forward into the sea of people and as he was just about to turn around and check out the rear of the plane his neighbour greeted him.

"Hello, I'm Martin, what's your name?"

Now at first Antonio thought it might be a foreign language but stopping to think, looking a bit blank at his neighbour he realised it was in fact English that was being spoken. He answered politely with;

"Excuse me?"

"Hi, I'm Martin, what's your name?"

This time the neighbour had spoken a lot slower and Antonio was able to make out the question.

"I'm Antonio and very pleased to meet you Martin."

Antonio probably wasn't the only one who could have mistaken the language for anything other than English as Martin, it turned out, was a born and bred English lad sure enough, but from Dudley. Antonio's English was very good but his only experience of dialects were that of the teachers he had had at school who by virtue of their jobs had spoken English in a very clear and understanding way. This accent was totally new to Antonio and would cause a lot of pauses in their conversations over the next twelve hours of their flight.

It turned out that Martin had been on holiday with his mother to visit his aunt in Johannesburg who had emigrated to South Africa some ten years earlier. It was the first time Martin had ever been to South Africa and with it going to be Antonio's first visit to England the two boys found they could find a great deal to talk about during the flight, one telling of his homeland and vice versa.

Martin soon realised from the way in which Antonio was describing his home, that he hadn't really been to the real Africa but more like London in the sun and there and then made a pact with Antonio that one day, when he was older and able to travel alone that he would visit Antonio and experience the Africa that sounded such a great place compared to the high rise City he had before then also had thought of as the real Africa.

The two new friends got on well and Martin was able to assist Antonio with the description of the meal they had been served. Antonio looked at his meal and his first thought was that there was no rice. He had rarely before eaten a main meal without rice. In Romanbasque rice is served with everything, with every meal and to eat a meal without it was somewhat strange for Antonio.

For their meal they were served chicken in a plum sauce, duchess potatoes, carrots, peas and a few mushrooms delicately laid on top of the chicken. It was followed by a tub of trifle and a fairy cake. All this in itself was a strange meal for Antonio to be eating but he thought this was the beginning of the new diet he would be eating in England so he had better just try and get used to it. After flying all night they were woken with a full English breakfast with orange juice, the first time Antonio had eaten this meal but he was unable to finish it as it was only a few hours previously he had eaten, to him a large meal and was still full from that one.

With the time taken for the meals and the sleep they had over night it was now soon that they would be arriving in England at Heathrow airport and the real adventure would begin. The cabin became rather busy with stewards and stewardesses rushing around to collect the remaining trays from the breakfast meal to stow them away and the collection of rubbish being done. The busy had almost finished when another 'Ping' was heard and the Captain announced that they would soon be taking up their position to land.

As the announcement finished the plane lowered at the front and they were now definitely on their way down back to earth. This happening made Antonio again grip his seat in the same way he had before when they had taken off from Johannesburg. Another slight fear came over him and the challenge of the unknown was once more upon him. Expecting the worst, Antonio eventually closed his eyes as they descended right up until the bump of the wheels was felt as they hit the runway and they were down and what seemed to Antonio running free along the runway at a speed that there was no way they would be able to stop before going straight off the runway at the other end. The breaks were then applied in earnest and the plane slowed to a very controllable roll and Antonio again relaxed and made a sigh of relief before announcing to his new friend that he had really enjoyed that.

Antonio didn't as yet know where he would be staying in England apart from that is, Bradford somewhere so he didn't have an address he could give to Martin but Martin supplied him with his and Antonio promised to write to him and to stay in touch so that Martin could visit at some time in the future.

Martin said they would say their goodbyes now as he knew what a mad time it would be as they started to get off the plane and go into the arrivals to collect their baggage. The two new friends shock hands and affirmed their promises to each other and everybody in the plane started to stand up and tried to get off all at the same time.

Antonio just followed the crowd as he left the plane and after some time they arrived at the belts where their luggage would be coming from. Antonio waited patiently for what was his luggage to appear, and he waited and he waited and eventually he could see his wrap coming along the belt towards him. He didn't have much but for a moment he did think that because of what it was, a mere wrap. it had been left behind and his few possessions had been lost. He collected the wrap and again followed the crowds to join what he was by now getting very used to, another queue.

The queue he could see ahead of him was separating into two lines and he could see above the lines two signs which said EU Passports and Non EU Passports so he took the queue Non EU Passports and shuttled slowly along behind the others who had joined this queue. His queue was going a lot slower than the other as each person was personally checked and their passports were being stamped so they could move on. It was some fifteen minutes before he eventually got to the front of this queue and he was politely greeted with;

"Passport Please?" came from the officer, hand out to take Antonio's passport.

Antonio handed over his passport and the officer checked it very carefully.

"What is your business here in the UK?"

Antonio answered that he was here to study and the official

looked to the back of his passport and saw that he had a student's visa and he reminded Antonio that he had only two years in the UK or he would have to apply for a further visa. Antonio thanked the official and was allowed through the gates and he was now in England.

Antonio knew that someone was going to be meeting him at the airport and he was to look out for a sign with his name on it. He walked forward for a distance and he could see a crowd of people that were obviously waiting for passengers to arrive off the flights. He started to look for someone holding a sign with his name on it and at first couldn't see his name anywhere. He walked forward some more and stood at the back, he could just make his name on a piece of paper being held up by a rather large woman who was dressed in a very African style. He made his way to her and announced;

"Antonio Thica, that's me, hello I'm very pleased to meet you."

The women greeted Antonio politely and introduced herself as Mrs. Carolina Mbundo and they continued to pass pleasantries for rather longer than Antonio was expecting. Mrs. Carolina, it turned out was from the Romanbasque High Commission and she explained to Antonio what he would be doing for the rest of the day and led him outside to a very nice car, which Antonio felt he just had to comment on. He was going to get into a Mercedes E Class 550 long wheel base and it was the finest car he had ever seen. Highly polished and inside it just smelt so clean and unused. The driver welcomed Antonio to Great Britain and introduced himself as Mr. Dennis. Mr. Dennis was a short man but at the same time very stocky. His smile would cheer anyone up and consequently gave Antonio a big grin on meeting him. They all settled into the car and made their way off towards the exit of the airport. Antonio turned to Mrs. Carolina and said;

"Such a lot of traffic?" Mrs. Carolina replied;

"You haven't seen anything yet, wait until we get into London and then you will see what real traffic is all about."

Antonio, as he had done on the plane glued himself to the window so that he was in the best position to take in all the sights of this fantastic place he had only in the past been able to read about in books.

As they left the main road from the airport and joined the motorway Antonio did start to get nervy as he realised the speed they were now travelling. In the past speeds such as these he had never experienced and as the nerves left him excitement replaced them and he really started to enjoy himself as he explored everything that he possibly could from his vantage point of the back window of this so impressive car.

As they drove, Mrs. Carolina would point out various places of interest to Antonio he was pleased to be able to see the places he previously only read about. He found he was able to ask questions from what he had read and was so pleased that either Mrs. Carolina or Mr. Dennis was able to give him very good answers.

Their first stop was to be the High Commission as the Commissioner had asked to see this boy that was so special in the letters he had received from the various people who had referred him to undergo his schooling in Britain. The letters had been very impressive, not like the normal letters he had received for other candidates.

It wasn't too long before they arrived at the High Commission and Antonio was led in and as they went Mrs. Carolina quickly introduced him to everyone. Antonio was a bit shy as it seemed to him that they had all been waiting especially for him to arrive. Mrs. Carolina took him into a very large room with chairs around the edges, just one central table and a high polished floor and asked him to sit and she would be back shortly. Antonio scanned the room and was able to recognise some of the pictures on the walls as coming from his home land. He suddenly thought of home and for that moment became very home sick, but this didn't last very long as he remembered why he had been lucky enough to be sent here.

A click rang through the room and a great door opened and Mrs. Carolina peered on an angle around the open door.

"Come in please Antonio, the Commissioner is ready for you."

Antonio stood up and with a little trepidation walked towards the great door and saw through the opening sitting at a very large desk the Commissioner.

"Come in Antonio, come in my boy." The Commissioner stood and with a flourish of one arm invited Antonio to sit down.

"Antonio, I heard some very good things about you my boy. Many people have stated your case to me and I must say if you hadn't had been granted the permission to come here I think it would have caused trouble in our country."

Antonio smiled and simply replied;

"Thank you Sir!"

"You have been selected to attend the University at Bradford I believe?"

Yes Sir" replied Antonio.

"Sir, I do have one question."

"Yes, Antonio, what is that?"

"At the airport I was told I had a two year visa for being a student but my course is for three years. What will happen when my visa runs out?"

"That is a fine question from someone who is obviously going to be a scholar one day. Don't you worry about that Antonio; if you maintain a good grade average and it is certain you are going to pass the course your visa will automatically be extended. The longest visa you are allowed as a student is two years and then we look at the way you have been on the course and I think everything will be OK but very good question. I hope you continue to ask questions like that as you work your way through the course. It will certainly keep your teachers on their toes."

Antonio thanked the Commissioner and then asked the Commissioner which University he had attended?

"Antonio, you would expect that someone in my position could say the name of a great University or even a good college in England but I trained as an engineer before going into politics and I was lucky enough to stay in my home town of Deirai at one of our own fine Universities. This is also my first visit to Great Britain and I have now been here for just over a year."

"As yet I have not had the privilege of travelling to Deirai but I do hope one day to go there."

"A lovely part of our Country Antonio and you must go there one day and enjoy the second City of our Country, and if I am there at that time you must visit."

"I would be honoured Sir and I am already looking forward to it."

With that the Commission stood and explained that Mrs. Carolina would look after him while he was in London but he must keep in touch and write, telling us of your course and what you are getting up to.

"Any problems you have Antonio are my problems, please let us know if we can assist you, I believe a lot of people are counting on you."

Antonio again thanked the Commissioner and turned and was ushered out of the door by Mrs. Carolina who followed him into the outer room.

"Antonio soon I will be taking you to where you will be staying tonight but first I have something to do. Can you make your way down the stairs and wait for me down there?"

Without answering Antonio walked to the stairs and made his way down.

At the bottom of the stairs was Mr. Dennis who was watering some plants when Antonio arrived.

"Hi Antonio, been to see the boss?"

"Yes, a very nice gentleman." Antonio replied.

"Do you drink tea or would you like a cold drink?"

"Tea please, I do like tea when I can get it." Antonio had tasted tea many times but this would be his first in England and thought of the great British tradition he had heard so much about. When it came, he was somewhat disappointed as it tasted the same as if he had made it at home, he didn't really know what he expected but he certainly didn't expect it to taste the same.

Antonio waited with Mr. Dennis for about an hour for Mrs. Carolina but eventually she came and all of a sudden was in a hurry to leave. Mr. Dennis led the way out to the car and in moments they were again travelling through the London traffic.

On the way Mrs. Carolina continued pointing out places of interest and explaining various places to Antonio and Antonio remained silent taking it all in and really enjoying his lesson from Mrs. Carolina who, he thought was a wealth of knowledge on this great City.

It took nearly an hour to reach the place where Antonio would be spending his first night in England. The car stopped and Mr. Dennis, as if by magic was at the door before Antonio had realised they had in fact stopped. He got out of the car and followed Mr. Dennis to the rear of the car to collect his wrap. He thanked Mr. Dennis, they shock hands and Antonio followed Mrs. Carolina up a long flight of steps, which led to the house he would be staying at. She rang the door bell and they both stood and waited. They waited a few minutes and then Mrs. Carolina rang again. As she did the door opened. Mrs. Carolina jumped back in a start and a tall slim white girl of about twenty greeted them in the most perfect Romanbasque. Antonio looked at her and then looked away as he could feel himself blushing at the sight of this young girl.

"Antonio this is Mary." said Mrs. Carolina.

"Hello Antonio very pleased to meet you, come in both of you." Mary said.

They entered the house and walked along a passage that had many doors off it and they walked straight down to the bottom of the passage and ended up in the kitchen. The kitchen, in keeping with the rest of the house was also very large and a big, very old table was sat in the centre of the floor.

"Take a seat Antonio, would you like a drink before you go Mrs. Carolina?" Mary asked.

"No thank you Mary, we will have to get going if we are to miss the main traffic." Mrs. Carolina replied.

Antonio looked at them both and questioned.

"Main traffic, they have even more than what we have just seen." The two women laughed and Mrs. Carolina said;

"You will learn for yourself exactly what it is like here Antonio but you can't compare it with back home at all." She laughed and made her way out of the kitchen and back down the passage, shouting

"I'll see you tomorrow Antonio, Mary will look after you, bye."

"Bye" Antonio replied and Mrs. Carolina was gone out the door and Antonio heard the car rev up and pull away.

Mary had followed Mrs. Carolina to the door and was now back in the kitchen.

"Have you eaten or would you like to eat something now, we will be eating in about two hours if you can wait that long?" Mary asked.

"I am fine thank you and I would rather wait until you eat if you don't mind?" Antonio replied.

"That's fine we will be about ten for dinner and you will be able to meet everybody. Most are out at work now but they will start coming in shortly." Mary added.

Antonio didn't add any further to the conversation as he could feel himself blushing again. Mary started to make herself busy in the kitchen and was opening cupboards and pans were appearing and vegetables were taken from cupboards and a whole load of chicken came out of the fridge. Antonio thought of how organised she was and offered to help.

"Give me a minute Antonio and I'll show you your room and you can get yourself settled before the others come in." Mary said.

"OK." Antonio replied and sat back down as if he had been ordered to do so.

Mary's minute turned into five, but as the minutes past a wonderful aroma filled the kitchen. Onions were frying nicely and fresh tomatoes were being prepared to join the onions in the pan. A teaspoon of some spice or other was added to the pan followed by tomato puree and Antonio was ready to eat now and not to wait for the others but he kept this thought to himself.

Once Mary had the ingredients frying she turned to Antonio and said;

"Right let's show you to your room."

Antonio stood and followed Mary back down the passage and up the stairs, then another flight of stairs and yet another before reaching the entrance of what was to be his room for this one night only.

As Mary entered the room a bright light filled the passage way coming from the very large window in the room. Antonio followed Mary in and there he saw he had a bed, a wardrobe and a table at the side of the bed with an ashtray on it. Mary opened the wardrobe to show Antonio that there were hangers if he needed them and said that dinner would be in one hour then walked out of the room and she was gone down the stairs before Antonio could even say thank you.

For a moment Antonio looked out of the window and surveyed the bit of garden he could see from this point and then sat on the bed initially just to gather his thought's before possibly having a wash and generally tidying himself up before going down to dinner and meeting the others. He sat on the bed, which was very comfortable and in fact the first sight he had had of a bed for over two weeks now with all the travelling he had been doing. He sat, thought, and in a moment was laid out on the bed eyes shut and asleep. The hour passed and a knock came to the door. Antonio didn't stir at all and the knock came again. The door opened and the person walked across Antonio's room and shook him on the arm. Nothing at all, Antonio just laid there totally unaware that someone was trying to raise him for dinner. The person tried again but nothing so they turned and left Antonio to feast on his dreams.

It was the next morning when Antonio awoke at about six o'clock. He opened his eyes and at first wondered where he was but he saw the large window and remembered he was in London. He checked the time and only being six o'clock he had a wash, tidied himself up a bit and went down to have dinner. When he entered the kitchen there was already three others there. They said "hello" and introduced themselves as Joe, Steve and Louise.

"You must be Antonio?" Louise asked.

"Eh Yes, that's right." Antonio replied.

Antonio was a bit taken aback as he could remember the cooking being started the last time he was in the kitchen but now he was watching people eating cornflakes. He looked a bit odd when Steve asked.

"Are you going to have some breakfast with us?"

"Breakfast?" Antonio asked.

"What time is it?" Antonio continued.

"It's quarter past six." Steve answered.

"Have I missed dinner then?" Asked Antonio.

"Quarter past six in the morning, sleepy, you have been asleep all night." Joe nearly shouted as he held his laughter back, for a while anyway and then he just burst out laughing and told Antonio about how he had tried to wake him last night but that he was out for the count. Steve and Louise started to laugh, which made Antonio eventually laugh saying;

"And I expected to have such a beautiful meal of onions, tomatoes and that chicken looked very tasty, so now I must settle for some cornflakes, I can't believe I have slept for so long."

"You must have needed it," said Louise.

"If you have some cornflakes while you're waiting I'll knock you up some sausages and beans in a while." She added.

"Please don't trouble yo….." Antonio was stopped mid sentence and Louise said.

"No trouble, get yourself a bowl of cereal and I'll just be a few minutes and I'll be joining you and I bet Steve will have some?"

Steve was a big eater and if it was available, he would eat it, just to be polite he always said.

Steve gave Antonio a little grin as if to confirm what Louise had said about him and Antonio grinned back.

Antonio was half way through his plate of five sausages and beans when Mary appeared and said something but Antonio didn't hear but it must have been about him as the others laughed.

Mary was all dressed up; looking very smart and she told Antonio that she would be taking him to Bradford and that they would have to leave at about eight o'clock.

"Plenty of time but we must get the eight fifteen tube. Tube, that was a new word for Antonio and he asked what she meant by 'tube'. Mary explained that it was a train that went underground and left it like that. Antonio knew what a train was and seemed happy with Mary's explanation.

After their breakfast the three new friends wished Antonio all the best for his trip and hoped he really enjoyed Bradford and they rushed out the kitchen door and just a few minutes later Antonio heard the front door slam and they were gone.

Mary was sitting at the table finishing off her breakfast and as she ate she made some polite conversation with Antonio preparing him for what she thought he would encounter when he got to Bradford.

She told him of the place he would be staying at and how she knew the people there and they were very nice and that he should be very happy staying with them. Mary finished eating and took her dish to the sink and just left it saying that someone else could look after the house today, she was on a short holiday.

Eight o'clock came and the two friends left on their way to the tube. It was a short walk but Antonio again commented on the number of people and cars. Mary just said.

"This is London" and that seemed enough for Antonio who didn't add anything to the conversation apart from;

"OK"

At the tube Mary bought the tickets from the automatic machine and Antonio looked a bit quizzed and asked;

"How does it know how far we are going?" being his first encounter with an automatic machine. Mary gave a suitable short answer and they moved on to the platform.

Now the temperature for London at this time was not the normal temperatures that Antonio was used to. Especially with it being the beginning of September but in the station, on the platform Antonio started to shiver as he could hear the wind travelling along the tunnels. Mary looked at him and told him that it is only two minutes for the train and we will be in the warm again. Those two minutes could have been an hour for Antonio, as by the time the train arrived he was freezing and the inside of the train didn't do that much to help him get warmer. He was just getting to a state of warmth when Mary said that this was their stop and made her way towards the door. Antonio followed her clutching his wrap tightly to try and improve his state of coldness as best he could.

They were now at Kings Cross Station and the amount of people rushing here and there made Antonio a bit anxious and he followed Mary with very short quick steps as if to speed up the movement and get out of all these people as soon as he could. They walked for what seemed like many kilometres along the corridors of the underground and then up the escalator which made Antonio feel as if he was going up to heaven at one point. The stairs went on and on and he wanted to, but didn't look down in fear he might get even more nervous than what he was already.

After that little interlude on the escalator, it must have felt like a respite to Antonio because as soon as they stepped off the escalator the people were there again and he re-enacted his short steps to basically hide behind Mary the best he could. He didn't think he had a fear of people but to have so many for your first encounter with real crowds was too much for him.

They made their way towards the main station and Antonio was rather pleased with what happened next, he joined a queue for the main line and he actually felt relieved at this, as if he had met a friend in this jungle of people. He stood patiently in the queue as if it was protecting him from all the crowds of people outside this wonderful queue which had become his sanctuary.

Slowly the queue made its way forward and then the guard was checking their tickets and they were through the gate and heading for their train. Their pace quickened as if the train would leave without them but when they eventually got to the door Antonio was pleased to see that their carriage was empty.

They boarded the train and took their seats. Antonio choosing to face forward but Mary was happy to travel backwards. They had a three hour journey ahead of them and so they made themselves comfortable and settled in for the trip. Antonio took up his normal position of looking out of the window so that he wouldn't miss a thing. This was all new to him and he would be taking in as much as he could. Mary settled back and adopted the snooze position. Just ten minutes wait and they were off. Next stop for them was Bradford and a completely new life for Antonio. He was nervous but really looking forward to it. He thought of back home, where the people of his village had done without so much over the years to send him here. He would do his best to make them very proud of him and he would learn everything he could to make their lives easier.

10

The train slowed at the same time as an announcement came across the tannoy to announce their forthcoming arrival into Leeds and Mary said that they would be changing trains here.

Antonio had enjoyed the journey that is, what he had in fact seen. There were times on the journey that he found himself waking from a doze he had just had. Not knowing the route he had no recall of what he had missed or for that matter any knowledge of where he was when he awoke. All the same, what he had seen he had thoroughly enjoyed and this he started to relay to Mary even before she had recovered from her coma like sleep she was awakening from after sleeping for the whole of this part of the journey.

The train slowed and very gently stopped. They got off the train and Mary stopped to look at the screen to see which platform they would have to go to for their connecting train to Bradford. This only took her a moment and they were off again with Antonio adopting his normal place of following the heels of Mary so as not to get lost in the crowd that had left the train with them.

Up one flight of stairs, down another, into an underpass passing the Buskers that Antonio tried to enjoy but stayed with Mary as she ploughed on forward, up more stairs and eventually they arrived at their new platform and Antonio hadn't seen anything except for the heels of Mary's shoes so as not to lose her in this, which was for him a maddening crowd that made him very nervous with such a volume of people that he was still finding it difficult to get used to.

They a stood and waited for their connecting train to Bradford and after what just seemed like seconds the train was standing in front of them. The doors of the train opened and again Antonio became apprehensive as a stampede of people left the train. He felt a tug on his arm, which was the signal from Mary to move forward on to the train. They entered the train and came to a sudden stop just after the entrance and stood, as if placed there as the train doors shut and the train began to move out of the station.

It was a fairly short journey to Bradford and they were soon off the train, through the station and outside where Antonio felt for the first time in the last hour or so that he was able to take a nice deep breath of relief as well as some fresh air.

They took a taxi for the short journey to the house where Antonio would be spending the next three years of his time whilst he worked on his studies at Bradford University and as he walked up to the front door he was nicely surprised to see through the window of the front room of the house, several people that seemed to be around his age. In London he had enjoyed meeting the people of that house but they were all much older than he was.

Mary led the way into the house after they had both been greeted at the door by a young lady, who unbeknown to her or Antonio would play a big part in Antonio's life over the next few years.

In the main room of the downstairs of the house Mary introduced the other three occupants as; Johnny, Margaret and the girl who Antonio unwittingly could not take his eyes off as Shirley. Antonio shook all their hands but lastly shook, but seemed to hold on to Shirley's hand as if he knew then she would be special to him and it was to start from now.

The new friends all sat down to get to know each other as

Mary had suggested and she went off to the kitchen to make them all a drink. Antonio sat next to Shirley and as the four friends talked as best they could with Antonio being asked questions about his homeland and background, answering in his very best English, Antonio's hand found its way into Shirley's hand and they both gave a little squeeze to each other and this was definitely the time when they both realised that they would become close and spend a lot of time together over the coming years. Antonio was also pleased that Shirley was able to speak some Portuguese.

Mary brought in the drinks and announced that she was ready for some sleep and would be leaving the others to get to know each other better.

Margaret suggested that they use this day to show Antonio around a bit and they all agreed and prepared themselves to leave after putting the now empty drinks tray back in the kitchen.

Antonio and Shirley walked together and occasionally would hold hands but all four of the new gang were happy in each other's company.

They walked Antonio down to see the University for the first time and he was most impressed at what he saw. He could see himself being very happy there. At lunchtime they introduced him to MacDonald's but as a lad just arriving from the African Bush found it to be very expensive as he was there with very little Romanbasque money let alone any Sterling, which currently he wasn't able to get as he would have to wait for money to be given him by the University and that wouldn't be for another week yet.

After using most of the day walking around Antonio's new home town they arrived home again and Margaret set about making something to eat for them all. Antonio was surprised when Johnny went into the kitchen to help her as from where he came from the men didn't do such chores as cooking. A number of things had started to prey on Antonio's mind as he sat, now alone in the room. Why was Shirley so forward with him? As back in his village Antonio had enjoyed the wonders of sex with quite a few of the village girl's, as was his privilege as the son of the Chief but it was normally he who would decide who and when he wanted to take this privilege and not the girl who would make the move to him. Shirley was very different to any girl Antonio had come across before and as well as showing Antonio that she was very interested in him, this he was used to, but Shirley also had started making a move on Antonio which he found strange as the girls in his village would come when he called but they would stay away until called to him.

He was running these things through his mind when Margaret came in to say that the meal was ready. He told her he would like to wash first and Margaret asked him to give Shirley a shout when he was finished. Antonio went to the bathroom, washed his hands and called out to Shirley. Shirley answered from a nearby room and told Antonio to come in. Antonio walked through the door to see that Shirley was just putting a clean blouse on, standing there allowing Antonio to see her perfect form before she did the buttons up on the blouse. Antonio thought to himself what a nice body she had and knew it would be his for the asking.

Antonio and Shirley went downstairs without saying anything and joined Johnny and Margaret to eat the meal. Margaret had made a stew which they would have with rice and bread. They had all built up an appetite during the day despite their trip to MacDonald's and so all tucked in as Mary entered the room. The four friends gave a little laugh to each other, all thinking the same thing; they had forgotten that Mary was there and Mary realised what the humour was about and joined them at the table.

Antonio was now a lot more relaxed in Mary's presence than he had been before and he told her of their day and what he had seen. Mary was glad to see that Antonio was now relaxed in her company and that they had enjoyed their day together but never mentioned the fact as not to embarrass him.

After they had all finished, Mary took on the job of clearing up, Johnny and Margaret had work to do for the following week to be handed in, Shirley helped Mary in the kitchen and Antonio went to the sitting room and sat in a chair. That was at 6.00 o'clock. The next thing Antonio knew was Shirley was gently patting his hand to wake him as it was now 10.00 o'clock and Antonio had missed the whole evening sleeping in the chair after the travelling from London and the tour around the area, his new excitements and expectations had really drained him. Shirley woke him and said that he should really go up to bed as to be fresh for the morning as she was taking him out again but just the two of them this time as Johnny and Margaret had to get their work completed.

Shirley led the way up stairs and took Antonio to his new room for the first time. He had only had his wrap as luggage so she had carried that up for him when he was asleep. Antonio entered the room and was very pleased with what he was looking at. He had been impressed in the room in London but this he sensed immediately as being his and he liked what he saw.

His bed was large and he thought, much too large for him. He had a wardrobe, a side table, a small table and a chair. He walked to the window and looked at the stars through the few clouds but other than that saw nothing due to the lateness of the hour.

He thanked Shirley and she wished him goodnight and left Antonio in his room, alone for the first time that day. He sat on the bed and looked around at his new surroundings and thought of what he was doing and thought of the hardship his people back in the village in Romanbasque had gone through over the years to allow him to come here at all. He felt blessed but very tired still and sorted himself out to go back to sleep.

The next day he was awake early, washed and downstairs a good while before other people in the house started stirring. He had helped himself to some water from the tap and as he was coming up for breath for about the fourth time Shirley appeared in the kitchen full of the joys of spring and this being September meant she was really ready for her day out with Antonio.

'What would you like to eat Antonio?' Shirley said.

'Anything you are having would be nice thank you' Antonio replied.

'I will be having toast if that's ok' Shirley said

'OK' Antonio said, and he went to sit down and waited for Shirley to prepare the toast.

'Anything to drink' Shirley asked

'I have just had water' Antonio said

The pair sat and ate their toast and Shirley had a glass of juice and as they were eating Shirley told Antonio of the places they would be going that day. Antonio was very pleased with what Shirley was telling him but didn't have any idea of what she was talking about but looked forward to seeing these places with his very own tour guide.

They had had a great day, which turned into a great week and they established their friendship many times in Antonio's bedroom where Shirley had stayed at night since their first full day together.

* * * *

Now it was time for Antonio to start his studies at Bradford University and he was ready, as being a knowledge hungry person Antonio had had too many days since last leaving the halls of knowledge back at his school and was ready to get back to learning.

His first day was to be logged into his memory for the rest of his life. He felt the power of education as he entered the university for the first time and he liked what he felt.

The initial registration over he was led to his first class by the arrows he was told to follow from the registration area. Shirley had split up from him shortly after entering the campus but he was very pleased to see her sitting waiting for him on his arrival in his first class. They had spoken about many things during their trips out but had never broached the topic of which subjects they were both studying. As it turned out they had both registered on the same course and they were both extremely happy about it.

They greeted each other in the same way that they had parted earlier that morning with a kiss and prepared themselves for what was to happen next.

As they sat quietly a small man entered the room, he would have been in his fifties they thought. It turned out that as the man began to speak; that he was Professor Steve Markinson aged 67 years who originally came from Rhodesia but now as he had done for many years lived in Leeds. He was quietly spoken but what he lacked in volume he made up for with animation of his hands that were used high, low, left and right to express his explanations of what, at that moment were quite basic things but he would go into overdrive as his lessons took hold. As he went on to explain, his passion was farming. It was not a job but something he felt very passionate about and especially for the third world and should be taken very seriously he explained with a look that would have had achieved an Oscar rating from any film buff.

'Are you all serious about farming in the third world?' he said in a quiet voice and to which he received no reply.

Changing his persona again, 'Are you all passionate about farming in the third world?' he bellowed out across the auditorium. The class awoke from their inactivity and sat up in their seats and;

'YES' they all replied as if triumphantly announcing their intentions.

Lowering his voice back to a respectable volume, 'Then we are all in the right place' explained Professor Markinson.

'We are here because we want to make that difference that so many people talk about but never seem to get around to making the difference, just talk'.

The man that was facing Antonio was the man Antonio knew existed but thought he would never meet. Not Professor Markinson essentially but Antonio knew there was a man that would have this same passion as Antonio knew he had but now he wouldn't be afraid of voicing it as he also knew he would be backed up by this man he now felt he had been looking for all his life.

Professor Markinson taught well and Antonio hung on to his every word, taking copious pages of notes in every class that this wacky, animated and very passionate Professor would be the tutor for.

He was to learn a great deal from all the tutors at Bradford but he looked forward mostly to the sessions with Professor Markinson, as he felt that he was so in tune with his teachings and wanted to be able to say that he was an Ambassador of the Markinson teachings.

Antonio soon became the class speaker, which came to him easily as he not only believed in everything he was being taught by this man but he had also thought this way himself for so long but hadn't been given this arena in which to express himself where he knew he wouldn't be shouted down. He listened carefully and took in all that he was being taught and was proving to be a very good student not only in these classes taught by the Prof. but all his classes that he was attending.

Antonio's relationship with Shirley and that of his education were both going well and his first end of year results were that of straight 1's across the board. His life was good and he was also looking to improve on this most rewarding time in his life by attending Public Speaking Classes and the Universities Debating Society.

He didn't realise then but he was having a good hand in his

own development for the life, he wouldn't have expected at this stage would ever become his destiny?

The first year was quickly over and the next two years were full of enjoyment for Antonio but he worked hard and his efforts were rewarded when he received a 2:1 result for his Degree. However, this was not all that Antonio had been working on during his time at Bradford. He had also learnt the art of making money by whatever way he could, fair or foul didn't really matter to Antonio as long as he gained what was the purpose of whichever venture he undertook, MONEY.

Whilst at home, money had little or no consequence to Antonio but here, he had learnt differently. He learnt very quickly that money was in fact power and the more he had the more power he was able to gain.

It had all started during his first year at Bradford when he was talking to friends about the little amount of money he was receiving from his bursary. The amount would have been more than enough for Antonio's basic needs but he found he enjoyed the company of others and mostly he required money to enable him to take part. This conversation was taking place while the friends, Antonio, Shirley of course, Damian and Collette were enjoying their, what had now become a weekly trip to one of the numerous fast food outlets in Bradford. Damian and Collette were studying mostly the same subjects as Antonio and Shirley and their friendship had began fairly soon after the term had started. Damian and Collette were a jolly pair who had grown up together as next door neighbours, who were also determined to save the world and were both hoping to work with one of the major humanitarian organisations when their studies were over.

The conversation led to Damian suggesting that Antonio could get a job to fit around his studies. This would bring in some extra money and give Antonio a taste of working in Britain.

As they spoke, Collette looked up from where she was sitting and there above their heads was the very thing Antonio should be looking at. There was an advert right above their heads asking for part-time staff for this very restaurant.

'Antonio look!' said Collette who was pointing up towards the advert.

'Here is the very thing you need, go and ask at the counter for an application form' she added.

Antonio thought for a minute and moments later he was back at the table with the application form.

They all gave a hand in its completion, Antonio signed it and took it back to the counter to hand it in.

A girl at the counter took it from him but before Antonio could return to the table to rejoin his company his name was being called out.

'Antonio Thica' called a fairly short, pretty young girl and Antonio turned to see who was calling.

Antonio Thica is that you that just handed this application in?' she continued.

'Antonio Thica, yes that's me' said Antonio.

He walked back towards the girl and she directed him to an empty table.

'So, Antonio is that what you like to be called?' the girl said.

'Yes, Antonio' he replied.

'I'm Gemma and I am one of the shift managers here, tell me about yourself Antonio and why you would like to work here?'

Antonio explained who he was and told Gemma that he was most interested in working here as he needed the extra money and he wanted to gain some experience of working with the public.

Gemma asked him the usual standard questions and it wasn't long before she offered Antonio a week's trial to see how he got on.

Antonio was to start the following night and depending on

how he got on he would be given another night and so on for the next week as a trial.

Antonio was very pleased with the outcome and returned to his friends to tell them all the news. They were all very pleased for Antonio and wished him luck. They were pleased that not only he had got the job but he was also able to save on at least one meal a day when he was working as the restaurant provided them with meals when they were at work but he was also was able to get a 10% discount when he was not working.

Like everything else Antonio had taken on, he did really well in his training and had no problem passing the weeks trial, after which it was arranged that he would work three nights a week for 4 hours each night and 4 hours on alternate Saturdays and Sundays. This arrangement suited everyone, albeit it did mean that Antonio only got to spend every other week on the FFN, 'Friends Friday Night Out' but they went to the restaurant where he was working and were able to talk to him from time to time, so it was a nice compromise for all concerned.

Antonio really enjoyed his job and didn't find any hardship catching up with his studies the nights he was off. He got on well with everybody and he was liked by all of his colleagues, especially one girl called Samonne.

Samonne was a native of Wulayaky and after getting to know Antonio became quite in awe of him. She was from a lowly village family, where Antonio was a son of a Chief. She would only talk when spoken to by Antonio and if he asked her to do anything, however menial; she would jump to it as if given a direct order by some sergeant major or someone.

Samonne was normally a quiet girl but able to talk as if for medals when asked a question, one thing she wasn't was shy, but just as you may often see in African countries, subordinate. She had a good figure, tall and extremely pretty that Antonio made no secret of how he liked her but felt he couldn't betray his affections for Shirley who he had now been having a relationship with for some 9 months.

He kept his distance, for a while anyway, that was until Shirley went away on holiday for a fortnight and after just one night alone that was enough for Antonio and Samonne was very quickly ushered into Shirley's spot for the whole fortnight. Samonne totally understood that when Shirley returned her position would immediately become redundant and dutifully accepted this situation as she had been taught back home in Africa.

One night Antonio was 'out front' in the restaurant, his job being that of cleaning the tables down after customers had vacated one of them. He was going about his business and totally unwittingly and unintentionally overheard a conversation between two men sat at one of the tables. They were discussing how they would really like to have sex with, of all the people in the restaurant that evening but Samonne. Antonio being quick off the mark immediately saw his chance to offer his services to arrange such a meeting and he butt into the conversation to say just that. He explained that he knew Samonne very well and with the right encouragement he would be able to organise her for them. This seemed to be a bit of con to the two men but Antonio continued to talk and they soon realised he was in fact being very genuine about the proposition.

'How much would it cost us?' asked one of the men.

Looking at the two men Antonio was soon able to weigh-up what he would be safe in asking for and said;

'I would probably be able to organise it for you for as little as twenty five pounds each if you are agreeable?'

The two men thought, conferred and one of them announced; 'twenty each' to which Antonio agreed and said;

'Leave it to me come back around midnight when Samonne is due to finish for the night and I will have it all arranged for you'

The men sort of thanked him but also told Antonio that

they don't like to be mucked around, stood up, and left the restaurant.

Antonio smiled to himself thinking of the extra money he had just arranged for himself and thought of the way to approach Samonne with the transaction.

'Samonne can I join you.' Antonio asked as Samonne had settled down at a table to have her break.

'Please I would be honoured' Samonne replied.

'Samonne, I have a proposition for you that will be financially beneficial to you.' Antonio said.

'I like the sound of that Antonio I could always do with some extra money.' Samonne said.

'Did you see the two friends of mine I was talking to earlier tonight?' Antonio said.

'The two in that corner?' Samonne turned her head and looked over and pointed to the now vacant table in the corner of the restaurant.

'Yes, that's right' Antonio said, and added that; 'they were two very good friends of his and they are leaving tomorrow to go back to sea for a while and they would really like some loving before they go.'

Samonne, being the way she was, instantly felt sorry for them and hoped that they would be able to find some before they leave, saying it with her totally innocent face on at this point, in a very caring voice.

'That's where you could help them if you are willing.' said Antonio.

'How do you mean Antonio?' replied Samonne

'Well you could give them that loving and I would make sure they make it rewarding for you' said Antonio.

'Are you sure it would be alright Antonio?' Samonne asked.

Antonio knew that the sex would not be bothering her as she

was a village girl and she would have been having sex for many years by now, normally for no reward at all, albeit with her looks she would have been chosen by the higher ranking men in her village.

'I will stay close to you and make sure you are looked after and I will see you home after' Antonio said in a very fatherly tone of voice, as if he really was considering her welfare. As if he really cared?

In her very subordinate way, wishing to please Antonio Samonne replied;

'If it will please you Antonio, I would not like to think of those two men going away without love in their hearts'

'Thank you Samonne, I will take you to them as soon as we finish here' Antonio said, and got up and continued his work as if he had just organised a tea party.

The meeting went off without a hitch, apart from the fact that is that Samonne had just been prostituted by Antonio and after Antonio had seen Samonne home as he had promised, and rewarded her with ten pounds for her trouble. Samonne was pleased that Antonio had given her the ten pounds, which would really help her out and she sincerely thanked him. Having little money to live on and counting every penny she had, but Antonio wasn't really listening but was already thinking of the next encounter he could arrange for Samonne and also the extra money he could make from this venture.

Over the next few weeks Antonio was able to organise several more meetings for Samonne with one man or another and even went further afield to get the men to increase his wealth using Samonne's body as his product.

Antonio's name started to get around in the more seedy parts of Bradford and his business increased to the point that he now needed more girls like Samonne to fill the bookings he was making. This didn't come as a big problem to Antonio as he used his influence over Samonne to pull in some of her friends to assist in the venture. The restaurant position soon became vacant as Antonio was building his business to the point where he didn't have the time to hold down a normal job anymore, and anyway he was making so much more money this way.

This venture continued for the full time he was in Bradford and the money just kept rolling in and somehow he was able to keep this quiet from his more conventional friends, including Shirley.

After completing his study course he was qualified but still hungry for learning and decided to investigate the possibility of doing some form of Military Service prior to going home to Romanbasque.

He spoke with the administration at the university and they directed him to where he could find out more about how he could follow this path of becoming a soldier.

11

The following year he found himself in Sandhurst Military College as a Cadet training to become an Army Officer, trained by the British Army to enable him to follow this whim he had, for reasons even at this point unknown to him.

His training went well and he enjoyed the learning but also the challenges, his attitude was changing as he was taught to give orders and how to make sure they were carried out. Unlike the other Cadets he saw the power in what he was learning and not just the ability of getting a given job done. He enjoyed the power of command and his results showed that he had listened to his teachers to enable him being awarded the converted Sovereigns Sword on completion of his training for 'Best Cadet'.

He was now a 2nd Lieutenant in the British Army and he was proud of himself but also armed with what information he had been given to deal with the rest of his life. What that would become he was at this time unaware but he felt good. He was to be given a tour of duty to of all places, back to his home continent of Africa, serving with the United Nations Peace Keeping Forces.

Not too long after joining his unit he gained promotion to Lieutenant and soon after was decorated for a heroic act, putting his life at risk to recover a wounded man out of the line of enemy fire.

He was enjoying himself in the Army but reminded himself that he must get back to his people from whom all this wealth of experience was coming from due totally to their efforts and determination that one of their village children would have all the advantages even if they could only afford for one to be able to have it, but also felt the need to have more money available, which the Army was not providing him with.

After just two years of active service he gained his release from the Military and slowly made his way home to his village.

It had been over three years since he had last seen Shirley and even though they had continued to write to each other on a regular basis their paths were never to cross again but he had met other girls, plenty of other girls. He carried with him an extra piece of baggage that he didn't really want to take with him, but he had no choice this time. While serving with the Army he had contracted syphilis, feeling the need for a bit of his own loving.

This was the first time he had contracted this disease but had been treated for many other minor diseases and ailments by the Units Medical Officer, most of which had been connected to one Sexually Transmitted Disease or another. His medical record was getting so bad that if he hadn't had chosen to leave the Army when he did, it may have been that he would have been asked to leave on medical grounds.

He returned to his village to very much a hero's welcome, and that without the village even being aware of his military service or even his decoration for bravery.

Their son had come home after being away from the village now for nearly seven years. He looked fit and well and no sooner had he arrived home he was putting a plan together to totally transform his village to take them forward into the modern world and restore his lost wealth he so badly missed.

Antonio's father was now starting to look very much like an old man and it was getting near the time when he would hand over the running of the village to his son but remain Chief in name only. Malanda Thica was so proud of his son and of his village for allowing him to do for his son what he had been able to achieve. His son now had a full Western education and was ready to lead his people.

Antonio wasted no time getting to work. He organised work parties to work around the village to put his improvements into place. He had access to the village's money so he was able to pay for the improvements that had to be brought in from the City. One day a tractor arrived pulled on a trailer that was also loaded up with other stores and provisions.

Antonio's plan was being put in place and soon a great difference was being seen all around the village. Housing had been improved, fields had many kinds of crops growing in them, a pump for the first time was supplying their water from a fresh water bore hole, medical supplies arrived and another building was erected to house the new medical clinic.

The village people were very happy with what was happening and they praised Antonio each and every time they saw him. Girls would swoon about him hoping that it may be her that he chose to be his wife one day.

Antonio was their special person and they all showed their appreciation for what he was doing for each of them in their own way. He would receive gifts of goats, pigs and foodstuffs and of course the girls of the village were at his beck and call. He was the most popular man in the village and the Elders decided that it was time for him to fully take over from his father.

Malanda was told of the decision and welcomed it. He was also so proud of his son and he was pleased that his son was being received and rewarded in this very special way.

The Elders, along with Malanda made the plans to transfer the title of Chief to Antonio and one day they gathered all the villagers together, including Antonio and made the joyous announcement.

'Antonio is to be our New Chief,' announced Malanda to all that were assembled.

A great roar of excitement went up and drums started to be beaten, chanting commenced and the whole village was in a very happy state.

The ceremony was to take place in three days and the preparations began in earnest to get everything ready for the great event. Chiefs from neighbouring villages were invited and gifts to the New Chief were being prepared.

The other Chiefs were also very happy for Antonio as they saw that what he was doing was also radiating out to their villages and as Cobuki improved their own villages saw improvement. It was allowed for them to use the bore hole to fill their water carriers, the tractor was loaned out to the other villages so their fields could be ploughed using this great utility. All lives were starting to become easier for not only the people of Cobuki but for all the peoples of the area.

On the eve of the ceremony Antonio visited his father, only to inform him that Chief was something he was not ready for and that he didn't want to go through with the ceremony the very next day. Malanda was shocked at what his son was saying to him and initially thought his son was joking but very quickly realised, that he wasn't.

Malanda asked his son if there was a problem that he could put right before the ceremony that would make things right for his son could take the honour of being Chief.

Antonio said that there was nothing actually wrong except that he didn't want to become Chief and hadn't wanted to become Chief for some years now.

Antonio explained that for many years he'd known that all this education that his father and his people had made available for him was too much for just the village, and he felt that he had a greater cause to use his knowledge on, and that was his country.

Antonio also told his father that he had dreamt for a long time of doing something great for his country and it was thanks to him, his father that he was now in a position to do just that.

He was proud of what he had achieved and glad that he was chosen to achieve it but now he knew he must leave the village and do what he could for the country and not just for the village and surrounding area.

Malanda looked at his son with a frown but this soon changed to a smile and soon he broke out in a great belly laugh.

'Antonio, Antonio' he shouted

'You have always been the clever one and you are right, you must go where your heart tells you to go my son, whatever you choose to do I will continue to be proud of you but now I must think of what and how I am going to tell the Elders and the people' Malanda said

'Thank you father' Antonio said, and promptly left his father's home and returned to his own to get his things together as he had decided he would leave the village that very evening.

Antonio packed and went again to his father's home where he said goodbye to his mother first and then his father before walking out the door and leaving his parents home for what would be the very last time he would ever see either of them alive again.

Antonio had left the village but that didn't help his father who now had to inform the Elders of his son's decision. Malanda decided to get it done as soon as he could and summoned the Elders to his home to speak with them.

Malanda approached the rallied Elders and told them what his son had decided and that he had left the village for the City. Now normally this wouldn't be such a big problem for Malanda as his second son would just stand in where his older brother was supposed to be but Antonio was the only son and heir to Malanda and he didn't even have a daughter to offer up as the bride of the New Chief once one had been selected.

At first the Elders were angered and not as much shocked but concerned at who would take over where Antonio had left off with developing the village into a more modern productive society, after all, he done so much and still had so much to do. The last thing that really crossed their minds during all of this deliberation was the fact that they didn't have a New Chief to ordain the very next day.

In the morning Chiefs and their people began to arrive at Cobuki carrying the finest presents a village had seen for many years. There were goat's fat for the slaughter, pigs, geese, donkeys, trinkets galore, fruits, vegetables and many, many other very special gift items fit for a Chief. One village had even brought with them a veiled virgin bride for Antonio to consider. All of his needs would have been taken care of, but he was gone, and Malanda was again left to explain the situation to a much larger gathering crowd.

He decided to take just the Chiefs and their Elders to one side and explain what had happened. However, most of them knew that something was amiss when the star of the day wasn't to be seen anywhere on their arrival. They all listened, some in disbelief, but all the same listened to what Malanda had to say, and he told them what his son had said to him and hoped they would understand. There was a muttering around the assembly and then one Chief spoke out.

'A son of our villages has gone to make this country a better place for all, we should celebrate,' he said and again a muttering went around and suddenly a roar of jubilation commenced and the jubilation continued into the mass of other people that had assembled and then continued as a party into the night and until very early the next morning with some continuing well into the next day.

The people were happy and intent on going forward and in their own way knew they would, and with the extra knowledge Antonio had given them, they could.

12

The festivities over, the men and women returned to their daily routines, working in the fields, hunting, cooking, washing, etc. The village calmed down and a bit of normality began to set in without the figure of Antonio being present and the village people seemed to be re-armed with his influences.

Since his return, within the village a lot had changed through Antonio's influence and knowledge, which Antonio had used to develop, and in most cases, 'change,' the ways and methods that the villagers were used to doing things, but did the villagers now have the knowledge to continue these ways for themselves? Time would tell and the results would be the deciding factor after all.

The incumbent teacher was currently teaching seven children, three from Cobuki and four from other nearby villages. Everything seemed to be rosy in Cobuki and this was to continue for several months with work continuing nicely.

Crop's' grown and ready for harvest, which called for all hands to the pumps to bring them in and make them ready for the trip to the City to be sold at the market.

One thing that the villagers didn't realise was, that when they loaded their carts for market was that they had loaded the same number of carts they had loaded the year before and the year before that.

The convoy of carts set off for the City and again jubilation was present in the village with great expectations of the results from their sales were in the air.

The quality of the crops that had been produced was obvious to anyone in the know; superior to the crops grown before, but the quantity was the same. Within Africa numbers are more often the deciding factor for the price you are going to receive, and not necessarily the quality, especially in the circles that these villagers would be selling their goods.

On their return to the village the men said they had seen Antonio and that he had told them he was pleased with what they had produced. He also told them that he was busy working with others to make changes to improve the country now and this news went down very well with everyone in the village. It pleased them knowing that their son was doing so much for everyone else after doing so much for them.

Antonio was working in the City Council where, with others, were opposing some of the ideas the current Council were operating and he was starting to make a name for himself amongst the people of the City as he had done in his own village. He was spending time out and about in the surrounding villages giving them the knowledge of how to improve things for themselves. He had made contact with a variety of agencies who were supplying various items of tools and equipments for the villages and training them how to use them. He was able to gain the villagers trust to the point that he again gained access to their funds and began to spend them for the benefit of all in the villages and of course Antonio Thica.

His name was on the tip of everybody's tongue and used frequently in daily conversations. It began to become inevitable that if Antonio was to run for a political career he would have such support that he would easily be elected by the people and this was to be his next step in his career.

He decided he would run for office in the next elections.

The elections were to take place in November, six months away and Antonio would use all of this time getting the people behind him. This he found to be quite easy and prior to the elections he formed his own Political Party and even long established members of other Parties crossed over to support Antonio's and his Party and the expectations for the City and surrounding areas.

His election in the City was recorded as a landslide and his Party took office and started to put their manifesto into operation. Antonio's control now was for the whole area, giving him access to all the funds that the Council controlled for the good of these areas.

His control was good and he governed the area well and his respect grew and his support spread. People from outside this area started to migrate into the area that Antonio controlled and his support grew even more. His name was now being used in the Capital City, Romanbasqui, and was being used in the Halls of Government, not with respect but looking on Antonio as a threat to the current Government.

As a City Leader it was part of the job to visit the Capital at times to attend meetings and be advised by the Government on policies they wished to be implemented in the Country. Antonio would attend and listen but then argue his own points and show proof of his improvements that were for the better of the people and not just for the good of the Council. His words would surround and echo throughout the Government Chambers and he gained support from members of the Government who also wanted to learn his methods. From these attendances he began to gain support not only of the Government officials but the people began to hear of the man who was changing the Northern Provinces.

Four years after gaining the Control of the North he opposed the Government with his own Party but lost by a small margin but entered the Halls of Government as the Leader of the Opposition. His Party had grown in strength and numbers but not enough to be able to lead the Country. For this he would have to wait another eight years. He worked hard in the following years but again narrowly missed the crowning glory of the Country's Leadership in the following election. He had the Northern and Southern Provinces just about sewn up but he had forgotten about the Central Region, which had an extremely large but very widespread population and that had lost him the Government's Leadership.

However, this election he was ready. Over the previous years he had sent his people to all areas of the country and he was now not only a 'household' but also a 'mud hut' name in all areas of the Country.

He gained the Governments Leadership in the same way in which he originally gained the Council Leadership, by a landslide. He was probably the most popular person in the Country, he was certainly the most widely known. Even a number of Politicians from the other Party were so impressed with him they swapped their loyalties to follow him after being staunch members of their own Parties for many years. Antonio seemed to have the Country's people all following him and he was enjoying the popularity and using it silently to his own advantage.

Having seen the other side of the coin by being educated in England, he for one in this vast Country knew that power came with money, which didn't mean too much to the majority of the population. Earlier it was mentioned how he was given control of the funds in his village, well not all of it was used for the villagers requirements, Antonio had made sure that his requirements were at the very top of the list. He also started to get control of other villages funds, a rather large payment also went his way in payment for the benefits he was bringing to that particular village. Just imagine how he felt now, he had control of the whole Countries funds; he must of course make sure he had his compensation for doing the job after all.

Antonio was slowly and very unwittingly making a very nice

nest egg for himself in a method that was in fact on the surface legal to anyone who wanted to investigate the funding situation.

Like other Politicians before him, he would create a scheme that requires funding, receive the funds and as long as the relevant paperwork is returned nobody checks any further.

It makes you wonder if there are any Government Schemes around the world being funded to better the Politician who instigated the Scheme and not the original people, the original Scheme, it indicated that it would. Maybe it would be worthwhile checking.

There might even be private Scheme funding which disappear without knowing that the actual Consultancy is in the name of the Politician who might have instigated the Scheme, or that he/she possibly is a silent Director of the Company concerned.

Antonio was now beginning to really prosper and the more assistance he gave to a certain village the more in turn he would prosper to the point where if there was any doubts that crept into any onlooker about the funding he would be able to make that problem go away by the use of his private funds, or Army, or just his private thugs, but what of his own village?

As the years passed things financial began to get difficult for the village of Cobuki. The money they were earning from the sale of their produce was good to the point of being much better than they would have earned from using the old techniques.

Antonio had taught them well and they were pleased with the results. However, the years had started to take its toll on the machinery, the tractor was requiring more and more maintenance and spare parts were costly to the point that it was eventually abandoned with the village unable to afford the parts. The main problem came from the price of the diesel it required, it was increasing to a price they just could not afford against the other more important requirements for the village. However, the plough was required as the old ploughs they had used for many years had gone or been burnt in one of the many festive fires they had held.

Consequently, the plough along with the tractor was being pulled by two horses to do the job.

The medical room had long been abandoned when stocks had run so low they could be kept in a box. The most devastating loss to the village was the time when they had to tell the teacher they could no longer afford to pay for her services and that not even being a wage in real terms, but pocket money.

Things in the village were on the decline after such a remarkable time they had all had from the teachings of Antonio that came from the dreams of his father Chief Malanda.

No problem! They are African they can now revert to do things the ways Africans have done them for thousands of years and revert to the old methods, easy!

Time has passed and a new generation was now running the village, a generation that have only done things the new way and the old ways having been buried in the past, so how is it done?

Sound too easy, doesn't it?

How many Westerners could revert to pressing clothes with an iron direct from the fire then? Not too long ago regularly used in the Western World. Or even to the more extreme, sit and watch a black and white television, no way!

The fact is the village is now going into decline and there isn't really a situation where they could revert to the old ways as not enough people know the old ways to be able to teach them.

Many people chose to carry on the best they could but mainly the younger ones made the decision to make their way to the City's or larger Towns where things are bound to be better, they all think.

Meanwhile Antonio had gained the position he was after and would not return to Cobuki again, he had no need to, the village had sacrificed a lot for him to be able to achieve what he has, but they wanted to do it, it made them feel good, anyway, most of the people who had given the sacrifice along with his father and mother were dead now, so, 'DEBT PAID IN FULL'.

Over the following few years Antonio continued to amass his private funds from nonexistent schemes, even taking a wife to enable him to amass twice as much from two different avenues. His funds were gathering nicely and the country was slowly feeling the pressure from the lack of funding going to where it should have been. The main thing for Antonio was, that when queried on where the various funds were he was able to show all the correct 'paperwork' to back up such a scheme that had in fact not happened. He had so many paid or for want of a better word, bribed staff working for him now they could always produce the proof that schemes were officially in progress.

The facts of the actual schemes or the scheming that was taking place was not known to the people but the effects of the lack of schemes was very evident to many people who were themselves, starting to suffer the consequences of Antonio's actions, or lack of them being the actual case.

His actions didn't initially affect him but the local Councillors around the country were starting to feel the reaction of their public. What made it worse for them is that Antonio would be seen on television or heard on the radio basically contradicting what his representatives were doing on his behalf. This would work in Antonio's favour with the people thinking that they as well as Antonio were being let down by the local representatives. However, this in turn gave these representatives cause to question Antonio, which in turn saw a replacement in that position and the curious public servant never being seen again. It was soon learnt by these public servants that to question was not going to be in their best interests, so many of them took the stance of being the same as Antonio and local activists began to disappear instead of themselves.

Again Antonio had regained the control of the Country he wanted, and for a while he was feeling secure in the fact that he was the true author of the country's future and that nobody was going to overthrow him, or what had now become 'His Regime.'

However, what all Politicians have to be aware of is that there are always the disturbances of the periodic elections that enable them to be able to continue having this control.

The elections were looming and Antonio would have to be re-elected to hold on to all he had amassed and the grand life that he and his wife were living to the full. A plan would be required and it must be that it would ensure that Antonio and his Party would win the next, very soon to be, election.

His team of Politicians started their campaigns and spoke the words and promises from Antonio's manifestoes, whether it was what they believed or not, knowing that it would make the difference between basically their life or death, as far as they were concerned anyway. It really didn't matter to them what the people who would be voting for them thought; they were only interested in self preservation and for the benefit of Antonio, it was working.

The elections came and went and Antonio remained in power and the luxury he had set-up for himself and the key to his success, his close followers who would do anything, not necessarily for Antonio but for their own benefits and survival.

This situation was kept very much in-house but Antonio's success was applauded around the world bringing imports, providing for exports, many jobs and acclaims poured in from around the world and Antonio's coffers grew.

Antonio would ask the outside world for various assistances and they would arrive and be received with thanks from Antonio but distributed to only where he said they would be to maintain his appeal throughout his country, or just sold to again improve the state of his growing wealth, this part also being unknown outside of the country and only to his closest confidants.

The many good things the rest of the world were told Antonio was doing, made him a very respected man throughout the world but in his country a different story was being experienced by a very large number of the population who weren't blaming Antonio for these deeds but his representatives who were not doing as Antonio was telling his people they should be doing across the media.

The situation for Antonio remained good and he and his Party remained in Office unopposed for two more terms until he was opposed not only by his methods being announced on his own media stations but also to the outside world by foreign media stations who had been invited to the country by his Opposition.

His struggling people were shown to the world over the airwaves until Antonio had them all cut off. He revoked all the permissions for the foreign media and forced them out of his country. He was also being blamed by the various humanitarian organisations working in the country and soon they were also forced out of the country.

Antonio then began to systematically close the country down to all outside elements and anyone who tried to oppose him was also forced to leave the country or face extermination by their own countrymen. This produced both a positive and a negative problem for Antonio. The people that stayed continually tried to oppose his regime. The people that left told the rest of the world of the regime and its methods. He was being attacked from both inside and outside his own country but still remained living in his luxury as his people suffered, most supporting his tactics and were being rewarded for doing so, but others opposing his tactics were suffering the consequences.

The more Antonio was opposed, the worse his tactics to stifle these oppositions would be. He governed by fear and threats of worse to happen to anyone who tried to oppose 'His Regime.'

A brilliant man, gone bad?

About the Author

Geoff J Gardner is the author who was born in Wales but now lives in England after extensive world-wide travel over the last thirty years. His 22 years service in Her Majesties Armed Forces and later as an International Consultant has given him travels taking him to all parts of the globe, many of which took him to a number of the poorest Third World Countries.